“Then You’re Not Mad At Me For Some Old Sin I Can’t Even Remember?”

Cassandra shook her head. “I don't doubt your memory lapse. No one could remember as many sins as you’ve racked up.”

Gard grinned. “Today I am a solid citizen, Miss Whitfield. Which brings up an interesting question. How come you’re still a Miss?”

“My personal life is none of your business. I’d like you to leave. Don’t underestimate me, Sterling. I haven’t forgotten how to handle a shotgun.”

Gard laughed. “Now you’re going to shoot me? Damn, I really must have done something terrible to make you think of murder. Did I kiss you?” His eyes crinkled teasingly. “Or maybe you wanted me to kiss you and I didn’t? Was that it?”

D0950548

Dear Reader,

For many years you have known and loved Silhouette author Robin Elliott. But did you know she is also popular romance writer Joan Elliott Pickart? Now she has chosen to write her Silhouette books using the Joan Elliott Pickart name, which is also her real name!

You'll be reading the same delightful stories you've grown to love from "Robin Elliott," only now, keep an eye out for Joan Elliott Pickart. Joan's first book using her real name is this month's *Man of the Month.* It's called *Angels and Elves,* and it's the first in her BABY BET series. What exactly is a "baby bet"? Well, you'll have to read to find out, but I assure you—it's a lot of fun!

November also marks the return to Silhouette Books of popular writer Kristin James, with her first Silhouette Desire title, *Once in a Blue Moon.* I'm thrilled that Kristin has chosen to be part of the Desire family, and I know her many fans can't wait to read this sexy love story.

Some other favorites are also in store for you this month: Jennifer Greene, Jackie Merritt and Lass Small. And a new writer is always a treat—new writers are the voices of tomorrow, after all! This month, Pamela Ingrahm makes her writing debut…and I hope we'll see many more books from this talented new author.

Until next month, happy reading!

Lucia Macro
Senior Editor

Please address questions and book requests to:
Silhouette Reader Service
U.S.: 3010 Walden Ave., P.O. Box 1325, Buffalo, NY 14269
Canadian: P.O. Box 609, Fort Erie, Ont. L2A 5X3

JACKIE MERRITT

REBEL LOVE

SILHOUETTE Desire®

TM

Published by Silhouette Books

America's Publisher of Contemporary Romance

If you purchased this book without a cover you should be aware that this book is stolen property. It was reported as "unsold and destroyed" to the publisher, and neither the author nor the publisher has received any payment for this "stripped book."

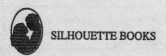

SILHOUETTE BOOKS

ISBN 0-373-05965-5

REBEL LOVE

Copyright © 1995 by Carolyn Joyner

All rights reserved. Except for use in any review, the reproduction or utilization of this work in whole or in part in any form by any electronic, mechanical or other means, now known or hereafter invented, including xerography, photocopying and recording, or in any information storage or retrieval system, is forbidden without the written permission of the editorial office, Silhouette Books, 300 East 42nd Street, New York, NY 10017 U.S.A.

All characters in this book have no existence outside the imagination of the author and have no relation whatsoever to anyone bearing the same name or names. They are not even distantly inspired by any individual known or unknown to the author, and all incidents are pure invention.

This edition published by arrangement with Harlequin Books S.A.

® and TM are trademarks of Harlequin Books S.A., used under license. Trademarks indicated with ® are registered in the United States Patent and Trademark Office, the Canadian Trade Marks Office and in other countries.

Printed in U.S.A.

Books by Jackie Merritt

Silhouette Desire

Big Sky Country #466
Heartbreak Hotel #551
Babe in the Woods #566
Maggie's Man #587
Ramblin' Man #605
Maverick Heart #622
Sweet on Jessie #642
Mustang Valley #664
The Lady and the Lumberjack #683
Boss Lady #705
Shipwrecked! #721
Black Creek Ranch #740
A Man Like Michael #757
Tennessee Waltz #774
Montana Sky #790
Imitation Love #813
**Wrangler's Lady* #841
**Mystery Lady* #849
**Persistent Lady* #854
Nevada Drifter #866
Accidental Bride #914
Hesitant Husband #935
Rebel Love #965

*Saxon Brothers series

Silhouette Special Edition

A Man and a Million #988

Silhouette Books

Summer Sizzlers Collection 1994
"Stranded"

Montana Mavericks
The Widow and the
Rodeo Man #2
The Rancher Takes
a Wife #5

JACKIE MERRITT

and her husband live just outside of Las Vegas, Nevada. An accountant for many years, Jackie has happily traded numbers for words. Next to family, books are her greatest joy. She started writing in 1987 and her efforts paid off in 1988 with the publication of her first novel. When she's not writing or enjoying a good book, Jackie dabbles in watercolor painting and likes playing the piano in her spare time.

One

The Plantation was easily the nicest restaurant in the town of Huntington, Montana, and the surrounding area, but as the meeting was set for midafternoon, there were only a few cars in the parking lot.

Cassandra Whitfield drove into a space, turned off the ignition and then sat there. The truth was, she hated walking into that restaurant to meet with Gardiner Sterling, and she wasn't positive she could bring it off with her dignity intact. What was he thinking right now? Assuming he was inside waiting for her, of course.

Swallowing a sudden spate of nervousness rising in her throat, Cass pulled out her compact for a final check of her makeup and hair. She had dressed carefully and taken great pains with her hair and makeup. Such perfection was not normal routine for her. In her own territory she wore baggy shorts or slacks and long T-shirts, secured her dark blond hair back from her face with a rubber band, and rarely bothered with lipstick, let alone all of those other creams and colors with which she had enhanced the contours of her face today.

But . . . she wasn't in her own territory. She was in Montana—where she'd grown up—and attempting to settle a simple contract that her father had made with Gard's father years ago. Thus far, although her attorney and Gard's attorney had been communicating on the matter, nothing had been resolved. Impatient with Gard's procrastination, Cass had finally instigated this meeting, insisting that it be held in a public place. She didn't want Gard in her father's home while she was staying there, and she certainly was not going to step foot in the Sterling residence.

Drawing a deep breath, Cass opened the door of her car and got out. Walking to the building, she presented an impressive picture of a confident, well-dressed, attractive woman with something important on her mind.

Cass's mind was full, all right, and unquestionably her thoughts were indeed important. But the past was a weighty burden, and deep inside of her was a fervent hope, a prayer, that she could handle this meeting with aplomb and even a little loftiness. After all, she was definitely not the smart-mouthed teenager that Gard Sterling had to remember from fourteen years ago, nor was she the easy mark she had become in his arms one long-ago night. Hopefully he had attained enough maturity and discretion not to mention that embarrassing chapter of their lives.

At present, Cass enjoyed a modicum of fame in the art world. Her paintings were not only beginning to sell well, but their prices were rising at a satisfying rate. Her own home was a cliff house on Oregon's rugged coast, but that could change, depending on certain factors. Her father's death three months ago had been unexpected and tragic, but making matters worse was discovering that she couldn't sell the real property she had inherited—the Whitfield Land and Cattle Company—without Gardiner Sterling's permission.

On closer examination, *permission* wasn't the best word

for Cassandra's dilemma. It wasn't Sterling's permission she needed, it was his decision on whether he wished to exercise the buy/sell option cited in that old contract.

Though Cass was proud of her hard-earned success, it wasn't on today's agenda for discussion. Gard probably knew nothing about her work, and she couldn't think of any reason why she would fill him in on it. For one thing, he certainly didn't need to hear that the sale of the ranch was crucial to her career plans, which had greatly expanded only recently. The renowned art shop and gallery in San Francisco through which she sold her paintings was owned by an older woman, Francis Deering, and for reasons of her own, Francis had put out an offer to sell fifty percent of the Deering Gallery. The opportunity had come up quite suddenly, shortly after the death of Cass's father. Since Cass had no intention of ever living in Montana again, it made perfect sense to her to sell the ranch and buy into the gallery. The problem was that there were other people also interested in that fifty percent, and Francis had said she would like Cass as a partner, but business was business and she preferred completing the transaction as soon as possible.

So did Cass, particularly since she understood that Francis was not going to wait indefinitely. That was why she had given up on the attorneys' slowpoke methods and arranged this meeting with Gard, even though she would rather walk on hot coals than see him.

She entered the Plantation and spoke to the hostess. "I have a meeting with Gardiner Sterling. Has he arrived?"

The woman smiled pleasantly. "Yes. He's waiting in the Peachtree Room. Follow me, please."

Cass's heart suddenly went wild. No matter how many sensible vows and promises with which she had saturated her system, coming face-to-face with Gard was going to be daunting. He was her most painful memory, the one that would sometimes sneak up on her during a restless night to singe her senses with humiliation and anger.

Her chin lifted defiantly. Today she would not be embarrassed and certainly anger was out of the question. The hostess opened a door. "Here you are, ma'am."

"Thank you." Cass stepped into the room to see a tall, lanky man in jeans, boots, a white shirt and a tan vest getting to his feet.

Gard was instantly confused. *This* exceptionally beautiful woman was Cassandra? The Sterling-Whitfield relationship had always been rather strange. Gard's father, Loyal, and Cassandra's father, Ridge, had been the best of friends, but their families had never meshed. Looking back, Gard could easily recall hunting trips, poker games, and numerous other activities with which Loyal and Ridge had occupied themselves. No one had ever thought it odd that their wives and offspring hadn't become friends, he realized now. They had all recognized each other, of course, and talked on occasion, but there had never been any real closeness between any of them, except for Loyal and Ridge.

But, to be perfectly honest, Gard would not have recognized Cassandra Whitfield if their paths had crossed accidentally. His memories of her were as vague as last night's dreams, and speaking of dreams, he felt as though one had just walked into his life.

"Hello," he said with a warm, welcoming smile.

"Hello." Cass's voice was as cool as iced lemonade. She glanced around the room. It was obviously one of the Plantation's banquet rooms, but only one table and two chairs were set up. There was a pot of coffee, containers of cream and sugar, a pitcher of ice water, two cups, two glasses, two spoons and two napkins on the table.

Gard gestured at the arrangement. "Would you like to sit down?"

"Yes, thank you." Her mind worked behind a smooth, silky expression. *He looks the same. How dare he look the same after fourteen years? Still outrageously handsome, with thick, black hair and those piercing blue eyes.*

Gard watched her gracefully cross to the table and chairs, and he sat down when she did. He wasn't sure he liked her hairdo, which was a twisted coil around her head, every strand tightly in place. Her dress, though, was great, a simply styled, off-white garment that looked very expensive to his eyes. So did her matching pumps and purse. She had dressed up for this meeting, and maybe he should have figured on a little more formality than jeans.

But, what the hell? He was a boots-and-jeans man, which Cassandra Whitfield had to know if she remembered him at all.

"How are you?" he asked politely. "It's been a long time."

"Yes, a long time," Cass agreed, also politely.

"I'm sorry about Ridge. Like my own father, Ridge died much too young."

"Yes, he did."

Gard frowned. She was so distant, as though they were meeting for the first time ever. A strange, elusive sense of something missing from his memory suddenly struck him. It had to do with her, with Cassandra. But that name. Had she gone by "Cassandra" in the old days? Somehow that name didn't fit in with *any* of his memories.

"Coffee?" he asked. "Or water?"

"No, thank you." Cass placed her purse on a corner of the table. The word *rebel* had invaded her brain and wouldn't go away. Rebel Sterling. That was what people used to call him, and with good reason. In her mind's eye were visions of Gard pushing his huge, black-and-chrome Harley-Davidson motorcycle to its limits, riding that machine as though he were an extension of it, hair flying, engine roaring, darting in and out of traffic on the highway, or cutting through someone's field at sixty miles an hour. And he drank. Everyone had known he drank. He'd been picked up by the law several times for drinking and driving, and somehow—probably because of his daddy's money and influence—he'd always gotten out of his scrapes. He'd been spoiled rotten by Loyal and doted on by his mother, until her death when Gard was fifteen. Fourteen years ago, when Cass left the valley, Gard had done whatever he pleased, and Cassandra felt he probably still believed the world had been created solely for his enjoyment.

Uneasy over the intense scrutiny she was receiving from across the table, Cass cleared her throat. "I don't have a lot of time, so I would appreciate getting right to that contract."

"That's why we're here," Gard replied, sounding agreeable. "But there's something about you..." He paused. "I can't quite put a finger on it. Did people call you Cassandra before you left the valley?"

"It's my name. Why wouldn't they?" But her cheeks got warm. People *hadn't* called her Cassandra, but no way was she going to remind this man of her old nickname.

But a peculiar thought was taking shape in the back of her mind: Gard didn't really remember her. Oh, he remembered the name Cassandra Whitfield, all right, and he certainly knew who she was. But he did not remember *her!* Which meant that he also didn't remember that night at the sand dunes.

Something deflated within Cassandra, her pride, perhaps. Certainly her femaleness felt the blow. The possibility of him having completely forgotten the most startling event of her own life hadn't occurred to her.

Her own memory insulted her further, the days and weeks immediately following that night. He hadn't called or contacted her in any way, and she had wept buckets of guilt and remorse and resentment.

Her face became a little harder. "Let's get down to business, Gard. You've had three months to think about that buy/sell option, and I need an answer. Let me lay my cards on the table. I intend to sell the Whitfield ranch, and it's immaterial to me who buys it. If you want it, it's yours. But you have to make up your mind. I can't put the property on the open market until you sign away your rights to that option."

With his eyes narrowed on her, Gard leaned back in his chair. "Why are you in such a hurry to sell? Doesn't your home mean anything to you?"

"*My* home is in Oregon," Cass said coolly. "I would like to get back to it, and your vacillation—to put it bluntly—is preventing me from doing so. If you say no to the option, then I can put Dad's property in the hands of a reliable real estate agent and stop worrying about it. That's all I want from you, a yes or a no, and I really don't care which it is."

"Have you read the contract?" Gard asked.

"Of course I've read it. It surprised me, I don't mind admitting. Did you know about it before Dad died?"

"I've known about it since *my* dad died," Gard said. "You know, that contract consigns you the same legal rights it does me."

Cass smirked slightly. "But I can give you an unequivocal no right now. I wouldn't buy your place under any circumstances." She leaned forward. "Why can't you do the same for me? Either you want the Whitfield ranch or you don't. Where is the problem in that decision?"

He was studying her, thinking hard. Both the Sterlings and the Whitfields had been well-off in his youth, and he would bet anything that Ridge Whitfield's estate—which Cassandra had inherited—was financially secure. The Sterlings hadn't fared quite so well. Actually, the Sterlings had done extremely well until Loyal died. That was ten years ago, about four or five years after Cassandra left the valley. Like her, Gard had inherited everything, the ranch, the equipment, the stock and the bank accounts.

But Gard wasn't a carbon copy of Loyal Sterling, and he'd been right in his prime, twenty-five years old and full of vinegar. He had grieved for his father for a while, but life had been so damned exciting that his period of mourning hadn't lasted for long. He went a little crazy spending money, chasing women, buying cars and motorcycles, drinking and carousing and having a hell of a good time.

Then, one day after four years of neglecting the ranch, he happened to be walking around outside, just wandering aimlessly and realizing that he didn't want to go drinking that night. He didn't want to drop in at any of his old hangouts, nor go after the prettiest gal in town, nor ride his newest Harley-Davidson motorcycle or drive one of his cars hell-bent for leather.

His eyes had narrowed on the weeds that had sprung up around trees and fence posts. The paint was cracked and peeling on every building. His father had never left any chore undone during his lifetime, and that day the place suddenly looked shabby and run-down. Two of Gard's hired men were leaning against the shady side of the barn, smoking, laughing and doing nothing but killing time.

Gard had stood there for the longest time, thinking of how far down he'd sunk for the sake of a good time. For one thing, he had no idea how much cash remained in his bank accounts, or even if there was any.

He'd broken out in a cold sweat, turned, walked back to the house and went in. It, too, showed the years of neglect. He was paying a woman to come out from town about once a month to clean the place, but Gard couldn't remember the last time he'd seen her. The kitchen sink, counter and table overflowed with dirty dishes. There were mountains of dirty clothes in the laundry room. The living room was littered with everything from clothing to old newspapers to empty beer bottles to foul-smelling ashtrays.

Some inner fear, brand-new and startling, drove him into the den and to the ranch's checkbooks. The small balances were staggering: he was damned near broke!

That was the turning point in Gard's life. From that moment on, he hadn't touched a drop of liquor, he'd sold every vehicle except one pickup truck he had to have for transportation, and he'd told his two hired men that they would work with him and work hard or they could pick up their checks.

He'd made headway. The Sterling ranch was again successful and earning an annual profit. Regardless, he didn't have the extra cash—a very large sum—that it would take to exercise the option in that old contract.

But he would bite off his tongue before laying that complex explanation on Cassandra Whitfield. Besides, it was none of her business, even though it was the reason why he hadn't immediately given her an answer on that option. The thing was, Loyal Sterling and Ridge Whitfield had had a dream of a united valley. To assure that only Sterlings or Whitfields would ever own any portion of it, they had devised that contract, which said, simply, that if either a Sterling or a Whitfield needed to sell out for any reason, the other party had first right of refusal.

That was what he and Cassandra were stuck with today, their fathers' hopes for the continuity of the valley they had loved so much. Obviously it hadn't occurred to either man that their children wouldn't welcome the same arrangement. Gard had every intention of living out his life on the Sterling land, but he had all but destroyed his chances of buying out Cassandra. She, on the other hand, probably had more money than she could spend in three lifetimes but had no interest in either the Whitfield land or Montana.

For some reason, Gard couldn't tell her that he just didn't have the financial means to buy her out. Thus, his answer to her question—Where is the problem in that decision?—was an almost belligerent, "The contract recites a 'reasonable length of time' for either of us to make that decision, which is the only reference to time in the entire document. As I see it, the only problem we have is with your impatience."

"You've had a reasonable length of time," Cassandra said sharply. Then, wincing at the tone of her voice, she added in a calmer vein, "Three months seems very reasonable to me."

"What's reasonable to you isn't necessarily reasonable to me," Gard retorted.

"Just what do you consider reasonable?" Cassandra leaned forward again. "How much more time do you need? I want this thing settled. I want to get on with my life, which doesn't involve twiddling my thumbs in Montana. I have work to do in Oregon." *And, hopefully, in California.*

"Oh? What do you do?" Gard was fascinated by the play of light in her green eyes. Along with that observation, Gard was becoming aware that Cassandra was trying desperately to keep a lid on her emotions. She was being polite when she would probably rather scream at him to get off his duff and do something about that option.

Mentally he snapped his fingers. That was it! She was a different person today than when he'd last seen her. Not that he could pinpoint that exact occasion, but the perfectly groomed woman across the table was not the girl in his memory, fuzzy as it was. That girl had been . . .

He smiled suddenly. "Now I remember what everyone called you when we were kids. It was Sassy. Sassy Cassie Whitfield." Cassandra's face turned three shades of red. "Hey, does that embarrass you? Hell, Sassy, you can't change who you were as a kid."

She was close to exploding, despite her determination to remain calm and collected. "I would think you would be the last person to be drumming up old nicknames, Rebel Sterling!"

He threw back his head and roared with laughter. "My God, I'd almost forgotten that, too. Well, you might find this hard to believe, Sassy, but Rebel Sterling is just another member of the establishment today."

"You don't look it," she snapped, and realized that it felt good to finally release her stringent hold on her emotions.

He grinned, lazily. "I'll take that as a compliment, honey. You know, every once in a while the old juices start flowing and try awfully hard to tempt me into doing something wild and crazy. But I'm a changed man, Cassandra. When that happens, I pour myself a glass of ice tea, sit on the back porch and watch the sunset."

That was too much for Cass to swallow. "Oh, give me a break," she drawled scathingly. "The day you drink ice tea instead of hard liquor and watch a sunset instead of the nearest woman in a tight skirt is the day I'll believe in leprechauns."

Gard put on a hurt face. "Sassy, Sassy, you must only remember the bad in me, and that kind of pains me. Weren't you and I friends?"

"No," she said flatly. "You and I were never friends. Look, Gard, I didn't come here to discuss your character or mine. I'll ask again. How much more time do you intend taking to make your decision on that option?"

Gard's thoughts would have surprised Cassandra. He wanted to honor the contract between his father and hers, if there was any way at all to do it. Strangers moving into the valley and living on the Whitfield place, doing God knew what with it, wasn't a pleasant prospect. Besides, there was something else going on in the back of his mind. The longer he delayed that decision, the longer Cassandra would be a neighbor. He wanted to see more of her, get to know her. She was the prettiest, most interesting woman he'd met in ages, and it intrigued him that they'd grown up within miles of each other, and here they were, together again after fourteen years. Besides, he wanted to remember that elusive memory that somehow seemed important, and if she scurried back to Oregon, it might forever elude him.

Deliberately portraying a man with a vexing problem, he rubbed his jaw thoughtfully. "I really can't give you a time limit, Cassandra. There are circumstances—a little too personal to explain—and there's my own place to consider. A merger of that size can't be decided overnight."

"Overnight! You've had three months!" Cassandra simply couldn't sit still any longer, and she got up to pace the room. "Give me some idea... anything. How about another week?"

Solemnly Gard shook his head. "Not nearly enough time."

"Then two weeks... a month. Dammit, you can't leave me hanging like this!" How would she explain this to Francis? God knew she would have to try.

"Leaving you hanging is not my intention, but I can't make this decision without further studying the consequences."

Cassandra turned to face him. "That's what you've been doing for three months, studying the consequences?" She sounded blatantly skeptical. "I honestly thought a face-to-face discussion would resolve the problem. Believe me, I never would have suggested this meeting otherwise."

Gard got to his feet. "At the risk of upsetting you more than you already are, I'd like to say something. You, Sassy Whitfield, are one very beautiful lady. What I'd really like to know is why I didn't notice that before you left the valley."

The strength drained out of Cassandra. The wretch really had no memory of that night. For fourteen years she had lived with periodic bouts of despising him, even while knowing that deep down she had *never* despised him. That had been the problem. She had suffered such an all-consuming crush on bad-boy Rebel Sterling that a mere glimpse of him had made her weak in the knees. After that night at the sand dunes, she had realized that her mind had been even weaker than her knees.

And he didn't even remember it.

Maybe she did despise him. Certainly, looking at that cocky grin on his face at this moment, despising him was as natural as breathing.

Walking over to the table, she picked up her purse. "Your opinion of my looks is completely immaterial. All I want from you is a decision on that option." Despite her determination to remain composed, her voice rose. "I don't know what game it is you're playing, but you won't convince me that you're not up to something."

"Tell you what," Gard said matter-of-factly. "Give me a few days and then let's get together again. How about on Friday? I could come to your place, or you could come to mine. Meeting here is kind of silly, don't you think?"

"A few days?" Would he really have an answer in a few days? Cass didn't want to be gullible about this, but she wanted this ridiculous situation over and done with. At least she wanted the freedom to call Francis and say, "The legal problems are over. I can put the ranch on the market and I'm sure it will sell quickly."

And now that she'd actually seen Gard, and survived, it really didn't matter where they met. "All right, fine. You may come to my place on Friday afternoon." Besides, it probably wouldn't hurt her case for him to get a good look at the Whitfield property. Lord only knew the last time he'd been there, and it was beautiful, in wonderful condition. Cass had kept the same employees who had worked for her father, and everything was in perfect order.

Gard smiled and nodded. "Fine. I'll see you on Friday."

Cass acknowledged the agreement with a slight nod of her own, then turned to walk to the door.

But then she made the mistake of stopping for one last look at Gard Sterling. The light flowing through the large windows behind him shadowed his features, but his height, his build and his long legs were all too visible. A choking sensation rose in her throat. Until this moment she'd been rather proud of her performance during their meeting, but now it was all she could do to restrain fourteen years of anger and resentment from spewing out of her mouth.

"See you on Friday," she mumbled, and all but ran from the room.

Surprised by her hasty exit, Gard almost laughed. But then the impulse died a sudden death and he frowned instead. There was more behind Cassandra's frosty attitude than that contract, probably something to do with the past. Gard groaned right out loud. What had he done to Cass Whitfield that he couldn't remember but she, apparently, had never forgotten? His youthful "good times" had caused him problems several times in the past few years, and he had a hunch the worst was yet to come.

He thought about that for a minute, then started for the door himself. Regardless of the past and its mysteries, he still wanted to know Cass better.

And surely he could make amends. Whatever he'd done couldn't be that bad.

Two

Cass awoke in a sweat, noticing on the digital clock next to her bed that it was 1:35 a.m. Whatever had awakened her eluded her, but now her eyes were wide open and didn't seem inclined to close again. Sighing, she got up and went to the kitchen for a cup of cocoa. Using a mix, she was soon seated at the table with her drink.

When Gard came to mind, she quickly put the blame for her interrupted sleep on him and the fact that she had agreed to meet with him on Friday. Then, to her intense annoyance, between her irritation and resentment was a memory: that infamous night at the dunes.

Groaning aloud, Cass put her head in her hands. How could she have been so stupid as to actually have made love with Rebel Sterling? She'd been young and naive, yes, but had she also been dim-witted? She had been at the dunes that night, sitting in the moonlight and thinking, just thinking. Then he'd come along on his motorcycle, and she had been so thrilled by the coincidence that she had started thinking fate had intervened on her behalf.

Dropping her hands, Cass picked up her cup with a cynical expression. If fate really had intervened that night, it had been a damned cruel trick, one she hadn't deserved.

Finishing off her cocoa, Cass rinsed out the cup, slipped it into the dishwasher and returned to her bedroom. Maybe she could sleep now, maybe not. But she was not going to spend the remainder of the night trying to second-guess fate. She had already played that futile game too many times.

It irritated Cass that she was just as nervous about seeing Gard on Friday as she'd been prior to their first meeting. Again she went through her mental list of dos and don'ts. At the Plantation she had come closer to saying what was on her mind—what had *been* on her mind for fourteen years—than she liked. Fortunately only a small amount of her ire had escaped, and she felt pretty certain that Gard had thought it was all because of his indecision about the contract.

There was irony in the situation. Without that old contract there was practically no chance at all that she and Gard would ever have seen each other again. It had probably never occurred to either his father or hers when they put that contract together that they had necessitated some sort of future relationship between their offspring. Without that accursed document, she would have put the Whitfield Land and Cattle Company in the hands of a real estate agent after her father's funeral and gone home to Oregon. The place would sell, she was certain, and for her purposes, the sooner the better.

But she was virtually stuck here until Gard made up his mind, which raised her hackles every time she thought about it. She wasn't in the best of moods when he arrived on Friday afternoon, but she managed a cool smile as she let him in.

"We'll sit in the living room," she told him, leading the way.

"The place looks good, Cassandra," he said as they sat down, he on the sofa, Cass in a nearby chair. His gaze went around the room, taking in the impressive, white rock fireplace and splendid furnishings. "Great house."

His gaze stopped on her. The "place" wasn't the only thing looking good; Cassandra's hair was down today, curled and swept back from the left side of her face by an amber comb. Her slacks and silk shirt were the same becoming shade of teal. She didn't look "sassy" today, she looked controlled and dignified and... remote. Gard wondered what had happened to the young girl who'd had a bright, witty retort for every occasion. He'd been remembering little things, events, moments of conversation, where Sassy Whitfield had indeed lived up to her nickname.

Of course, in those days he was usually half-sloshed, and even those facts he did remember had blurred edges.

"Would you like something to drink?" Cass asked with a hint of snideness. Naturally he would choose a cocktail of some sort.

"Wouldn't mind a cup of coffee," Gard replied smoothly, realizing that she'd expected a completely different answer. A chuckle remained inward and silent, but he truly enjoyed the startled expression on her face.

"Coffee? I'll get it." Cass rose and left the room. Gard got up and walked around, pausing to admire knickknacks on tables and a glass case containing a collection of porcelain figurines. Then the painting over the fireplace caught his eye, and he moved closer to inspect it. It took a moment to grasp its subject, and even then he wasn't sure if his interpretation was correct. It appeared to be a garden. The colors were wispy and dreamlike, and the foliage and flowers—if that's what they were—were oddly depicted and even distorted. Nowhere could he pick out a rose, for example, or a carnation, and yet he had the impression of a dozen varieties of flowers. He was no connoisseur of oil paintings, of any kind of art, for that matter, and yet he felt this was a good piece of work.

Then he spotted the initials in the lower right corner of the painting—CW—and comprehension dawned. "Well, I'll be damned," he mumbled under his breath.

Cass returned with a tray. Gard turned. "Are you this CW?"

"It's one of mine, yes." Calmly Cass poured coffee into two cups. She had no desire or intention to discuss her work with Gard Sterling. "Please... sit down and have your coffee."

"Thanks." Gard sat and accepted the cup of coffee, but he was still thinking about that painting. "Is that what you do in Oregon, or is oil painting just a hobby?"

Cass heaved a long-suffering sigh. "Gard, I don't want to talk about me. I really don't want to talk about you, either, except for one point. Have you come to a decision on that option?"

His eyes narrowed on her over his cup. "You don't like me, do you? Why not, Cassandra? What did I do to make you dislike me? I know something happened, but I can't remember it for the life of me. I've tried since the other day at the Plantation, but I can't come up with anything. You obviously remember what it was, so why don't you fill me in on it?"

The thought of sitting here and calmly narrating that night at the sand dunes nearly undid Cass. Her hand was suddenly shaking, and to avoid spilling coffee all over her own lap, she placed her cup on the table to the right of her chair.

"It seems to me that you are looking for ways to avoid discussing that option," she said accusingly. "I am not going to talk about old times with you, Gard, neither the good nor the bad. Just give me a straight answer. Have you made that decision?"

The small crack in her rigid self-control made him wonder if he couldn't widen it. "Then it wasn't all bad? With you and me, there were also some good times?"

Cass's anger erupted. She jumped to her feet. "You may as well leave. It's perfectly obvious that you're no closer to a decision on that option than you were at our first meeting." Her eyes flashed angrily. "I won't be played with, Gardiner. I think you've had more than enough time to 'study the consequences,' and just maybe a judge will agree with me."

Gard finished drinking the coffee in his cup, slowly enough that Cass wanted to screech at him, then stood up and brought the empty cup to the same table on which Cass had placed hers. "Seems to me that you're getting pretty riled up over nothing," he said with annoying calmness. "As for playing with you, Sassy Whitfield, a legal battle isn't my idea of fun."

He was standing right in front of her, and she vowed not to back away no matter what he did. This was *her* house, and this whole mess was his fault. "A legal battle is what you're going to get, if you don't make that decision," she said, putting it forcefully.

"Know what I think, Sassy, honey? I think you're mad at me for something that has nothing to do with that contract."

"That's absurd! I told you I want to clean things up here so I can return to my own home."

"Then you're *not* mad at me for some old sin I can't even remember?"

Cass's lips thinned. "I don't doubt your memory lapse. No one could remember as many sins as you've racked up. The list is probably still growing."

Gard grinned. "Today I am a solid citizen, Miss Whitfield. Which brings up an interesting question. How come you're still a Miss?"

"You nervy..." She stopped short of an insulting name. "My personal life is none of your business! I'd like you to leave. Don't underestimate me, Sterling. I haven't forgotten how to handle a shotgun."

Gard laughed. "Now you're going to shoot me? Damn, I really must have done something terrible to make you think of murder. Did I kiss you?" His eyes crinkled teasingly. "Or maybe you wanted me to kiss you and I didn't? Was that it?"

That was all Cass could take. Her anger exploded. "You conceited, amoral egomaniac! Get the hell out of my house! Any future communication about that contract will be between our lawyers. I will not tolerate any more of—"

The rest of her words were trapped in her throat. Gard had grabbed her and kissed her so fast, she hadn't seen it coming. His arms held her in place, and his mouth moved on hers with complete and utter possession. Her fury was so intense, it nearly burst through her skin, but there wasn't any way to break away. She tried all the tricks, the wriggling, the stamping on his toes, the growled, unintelligible invectives. If her hands were free, she would yank out every hair on his head. But her hands weren't free; they were trapped at her sides by the strength of his brawny arms.

And then it began happening, a deeply rooted inner response to his heat and power. To him, to Gard Sterling, the last man in the world she wanted to feel anything for.

Gard finally broke the kiss and lifted his head. His eyes contained a slightly puzzled cast. "Kissing you feels kind of familiar. Should it?"

"You're disgusting!" Internally Cass was a mass of quivering ambiguities. How dare he kiss her? But worse than his crime was her own; although she had shown nothing of what she'd felt during that kiss, she had liked it way too much.

The word *disgusting* hit Gard hard. He dropped his arms and took a backward step. "Guess I'd better apologize. I don't know what came over me."

Cass was trembling. "You haven't changed an iota. You still do whatever comes to your mind and to hell with the consequences. Most people have grown up by the time they reach your age. Apparently you haven't."

Gard was feeling a little silly. He hadn't grabbed a woman and forced a kiss on her since... since... Hell, had he *ever* forced a kiss on a woman?

Still, however foolish he felt, wasn't Cassandra overreacting? She was genuinely furious, making truly cutting remarks, casting aspersions not only on his behavior in the past but on the kind of man he was today.

His voice became noticeably cooler. "I have grown up, lady, but I'm beginning to wonder about you. You're just waiting to pounce on whatever I say or do, and—"

Cass broke in. "I suppose kissing a woman without any warning is adult conduct? And don't waste your time wondering about me, not in any context. You and I wouldn't be having these abominable meetings if it weren't for that despicable contract, and I have to question where your father's and mine's good sense was when they devised such a... a ludicrous agreement."

"It was a damned good agreement in their time," Gard growled. "And it's still good. Let me ask you this. Why do you feel like you have to hang around until I make a decision? Go on back to Oregon, if that's what you're so anxious to do. You've got capable employees. Let them take care of the place. They probably know a hell of a lot more about it than you do, anyway."

Cass's lip curled. "I neither want nor need advice from you about how I should handle my life, Gard Sterling. I'm staying right here until you do something about that option, and if you don't shake your fanny and get it done in the very near future, I'm going to start legal proceedings to *force* a decision out of you."

Smugly, Gard folded his arms. "Why don't you do that? You'll discover one thing about me, Sassy Whitfield. I don't take kindly to threats, and I guarantee that if you bring this to the courts, I'll have my lawyers drag it out so long, you and I will both be too old to care *who* owns the land in this valley by the time it's settled."

Cass's anger was shrinking, becoming less general and thus better defined. As infuriating as it was, Gard was not going to be bullied into a quick decision, nor was the threat of a lawsuit going to speed him up. She had vowed to remain cool and collected during this meeting, and instead had behaved like a shrew.

But why had he kissed her? And why had she liked it, when she was so opposed to everything Gard Sterling and every other freewheeling, skirt-chaser represented? That's what he'd been fourteen years ago, and he'd proved this afternoon that he was exactly the same, no matter how vociferously he claimed to be a respectable citizen these days.

The result of this second dismal meeting was that she had still gained no ground on that option. Maybe the only positive thing that *had* come out of it was the knowledge that he was going to take his own sweet time and she could like it or lump it. It was a frustrating moment, because she could almost see her chance to buy into the Deering Gallery flying out the window.

Still, she would do no more shouting or accusing. Gard Sterling always had been as obstinate as they came, and she would bet anything that the harder she pushed, the more stubborn he would become.

"Well," she said calmly, seating herself with an air of regained self-possession that surprised Gard. "It appears that we've reached an impasse," she said. "How do you propose we deal with that?" She sent him an innocent-eyed glance, and the essence of her expression struck Gard about four inches below his belt buckle. As insulting as Cassandra "Sassy" Whitfield could be, she was as sexy as any woman he'd ever met. A thought wormed its way into his mind and dug in hard and deep, as though entrenching itself permanently. *I want her. Dammit, I want her!*

Clearing his suddenly clogged throat, Gard approached the sofa and gingerly sat down. There was an ache in his groin that he knew wouldn't be appeased today, though he vowed to cure that affliction in the very near future. In the meantime, he had to make friends with Cassandra... somehow.

"I'm not sure our situation should be labeled an impasse," he said cautiously. "But, of course, we do have to find a way around it. As I said the other day, Cassandra, I need a little more time to study the sensibility and financial implications of buying you out." He'd said no such thing—he'd talked about studying the consequences—but Cass merely nodded her acknowledgment. "Obviously," Gard continued, "time is more important to you than it is to me. I don't have anywhere to go and you do. There's one thing I need to do before reaching a conclusion, and that's to take an in-depth look at the Whitfield ranch."

You snake! "Are you saying you're no longer familiar with this ranch?" Cassandra asked.

"That's it, exactly. I used to drop in and talk to Ridge once in a while, but I never got beyond the buildings."

"So what you'd like to do is check the land?" *You big phony. Whitfield land is no different than Sterling land, and you know it as well as you know your own name!* He was stalling for God knew what reason, but what choice did she have but to play along? If she could get an answer out of him in a week or so, she would do almost anything.

"Do you have any objections to showing me around?" Gard asked casually.

Cass made a small throat-clearing sound. He didn't need her "showing him around," the rat. He could get in his pickup or on a horse and see everything there was to see without her company. So...what was in the back of his devious mind? Another kiss? *More* than kisses?

She would never get over him not remembering that night at the sand dunes, and if he had any foolish ideas about luring her into bed, he was in for a rude awakening. How could she have liked that rough, overbearing kiss he'd given her a few minutes ago? Had she momentarily lost her senses?

Well, it was the last kiss between them, make no mistake, she vowed.

"When would you like to begin your inspection?" she asked in a smooth-as-honey voice.

Gard blinked. "Um...the sooner the better, I suppose. Are you free tomorrow?"

"Free as the breeze. Tomorrow, then? What time?"

"Might as well get an early start. Seven?"

"Make it eight."

"Fine." It was obviously time he left, though he would have thoroughly enjoyed spending the rest of the day sitting on Cassandra's sofa and looking at her in that pretty teal outfit. He got to his feet. "Let's do it on horseback."

"Do it?" Cass's face turned crimson. He hadn't meant *do it,* for pity's sake, he'd meant inspect the ranch!

Gard wanted to laugh so badly, his insides cramped and hurt. He'd "do it" on horseback, or any other place she could name, if "doing it" was what she wanted. It was an exciting goal to contemplate.

"Unless you don't ride anymore," he said with a completely straight face.

Was that another innuendo? Cass had to clamp her teeth together to stop herself from shrieking a vile name at him. But then a better idea came to mind and she smiled with all of the femaleness she could muster. "I...ride a lot," she said in a deliberately husky voice. "I love...riding."

Gard nearly choked. "Good...that's good. Uh, I'll ride over on my horse in the morning."

"And I'll have mine saddled and ready to go." Cass stood up. "I'll show you out."

They walked to the front door, which Cass opened. "Thank you for coming."

"You're welcome." Gard walked out and heard the door close behind him. Dazed, he made his way to his pickup, got in and then sat there. What a woman! One minute she acted as though she'd like to sock him and the next as though she'd like to... Dare he think *ride him?*

His teeth were gritted together as he drove away. She was still sassy, still unpredictable, and, Lord, was she exciting!

He could hardly wait for tomorrow morning.

Cass spent the evening on the telephone, talking first to her lawyer at his home in Billings, then to Francis in California. The two conversations were startlingly similar.

"Sterling's stalling and I don't know why. Now he wants to inspect the ranch, which is utterly ridiculous," Cass said.

"Maybe he doesn't have the money to buy you out and can't or won't admit it."

"That's not it," Cass denied. "The Sterlings were always very well-off. No, it's something else." With Francis, she went a little further. "He's an arrogant pain in the neck, Francis, playing some kind of silly game with me."

"Have you told him why you want to sell so badly?" Francis asked in her naturally gravelly voice.

"I doubt very much if it would change anything." Cass hadn't shared with Francis her surprise at the modest amount of cash in her father's estate. Selling the ranch was really her only means of buying into the gallery, as Francis had made one thing very clear: she would not sell that fifty percent for anything but cash. "You'd have to know Gardiner Sterling as I do to know what I mean," Cass added. "He's completely self-centered, and my having an urgent need to sell wouldn't impress him in the least."

"Please keep me informed, Cass. I don't want to put additional pressure on you, considering what you've been through, losing your father and all, but...well, I think you understand my point of view."

"I do, Francis, and I appreciate your patience, believe me. Maybe—I'm hoping, at least—to know more by the end of the week. I'll call."

* * *

In bed later, Cass tried again to figure out Gard's dawdling with that option. It was such a simple decision, either he wanted the Whitfield ranch or he didn't.

Her thoughts crept elsewhere. Could his procrastination possibly have something to do with her? Maybe he did remember that night at the dunes and what came after, and maybe he didn't know how to apologize. After all, hadn't he kissed her without the slightest provocation?

Cass's heart beat faster. What if that was it? What if Gard remembered that incredible, starry night, and hoped to bring them to that same point again? Men were sometimes so peculiar and closemouthed about emotions and feelings. After all, it wasn't impossible that he wanted to keep her in Montana, was it? Maybe deliberately delaying a decision on that option was his method of doing it.

A sigh lifted Cass's chest. There were too many holes in that theory to put much stock in it. First of all, wasn't she forgetting how wild and reckless Rebel Sterling had been fourteen years ago? And that he'd arrived at the dunes half-drunk and with a six-pack of beer to finish the job? It had probably been just another night to him, and why should it stand out from so many others? He didn't remember it at all, and she may as well stop thinking like a schoolgirl.

Cass's own memory of that night was suddenly so acute she couldn't lie still. Throwing back the covers, she got out of bed. With her arms curled around herself she paced the dark bedroom. Why did it still hurt after so long? she asked herself. She'd had men friends since, and yet that episode with Gard was the most unforgettable experience of her life.

It was also the most regrettable, she reminded herself. She had behaved badly that night, drinking beer with him, giggling over silly remarks, just so thrilled to be with him that she forgot every standard she ordinarily lived by.

But she had paid for it in the following weeks, paid for it every time she caught sight of him, every time he barely acknowledged that he even knew her with a nod or a casual hello. At the time it hadn't occurred to her that he simply didn't remember what had happened at the dunes, and she had interpreted every snub and slight in the most painful way possible. She still hadn't considered a memory lapse until seeing Gard again, and now, instead of feeling miserable about it, she should be grateful he didn't remember.

Cass returned to her bed and pulled the covers up to her chin. She was grateful, she told herself with teeth-gritting determination. Probably the worst thing that could happen in her present circumstances was for Gard to suddenly develop total recall.

Sighing heavily, she turned over and closed her eyes.

Riding beside Gard was discomfiting for Cass. She hadn't lied to him about loving to ride horses, and she had done quite a bit of riding during the last month. But riding alone and riding with Gard Sterling for a companion were two very different activities.

Still, she was trying with every cell in her body and brain to appear composed and nonplussed. The day was bright and sunny, with very little breeze. Starting out that morning, Cass had asked Gard what he wanted to see first. He had named the springs and creeks, which would have made very good sense if he'd been a stranger and unfamiliar with the valley's water sources.

Nevertheless, they rode to each of the ranch's three springs, where Gard dismounted, walked around and checked every little thing, such as the drainage runoff, the depth and temperature of the water, and the foliage around it. He was putting on some kind of show, Cass felt, irritated by his ridiculous attentiveness to details that were perfectly obvious to anyone with a lick of ranching sense.

They then followed each of the two creeks from one end of Whitfield land to the other. Anytime they came close to the cattle, Gard gave the animals a long look and, periodically, he dismounted to inspect the grass, actually breaking off handfuls and in several instances, tasting it.

Around noon Cass mentioned the sandwiches she had made that morning, having known instinctively that Gard was going to keep her out on the range past lunchtime. Which, of course, was merely another irritating aspect of the game he was playing and she was putting up with to get this ludicrous charade over and done with.

"You packed a lunch?" Gard looked pleased.

"Nothing fancy. Just some sandwiches." They were wrapped in aluminum foil and residing in her saddlebag, and by now they were probably overheated and soggy. Still, she was hungry and even a soggy sandwich would taste good.

Gard pointed ahead to a copse of trees and brush. "Let's get out of the sun to eat."

"Fine." Actually, getting out of the *saddle* was reaching the necessary stage for Cass. Four hours of riding was a mite more than she was used to, and she was feeling the long ride in her thighs and back.

They reached the trees and got down. Cass wanted to moan with relief, but managed to stifle the impulse. Gard, she noted, didn't seem to be the least bit tired.

She opened her saddlebag and removed the sandwiches, placing them on a grassy spot along with her canteen of water.

Gard sat down with his back against a tree near the wrapped sandwiches. He smiled at her and she did her best to smile back.

"It isn't much, but dig in," she told him, lowering herself to the grass.

They each took a sandwich and began eating. Gard removed his hat and laid it on the grass next to him. "Nice out here. Thanks for thinking of bringing along lunch."

"Such as it is, but you're welcome." Cass swallowed a bite. "Have you seen enough to make that decision?"

"Well...I've been thinking of that high ridge at the western perimeter of your land, Cassandra. You must remember the spot. Anyway, we had an extremely heavy runoff this spring—about twenty feet of snow in the mountains last winter—and I've been wondering how it affected that ridge. It was always a natural boundary between Whitfield land and forest service property, as I recall."

Cass stared at him. "Even if the ridge was entirely wiped out, what possible difference could it make to your decision?"

"We could be talking about some major environmental damage, Cassandra."

She spoke sarcastically. "I'm sure Dad would have told me if melting snow had washed away a ridge of land that was at least forty feet higher than the valley floor, Gard."

Gard shoved the last piece of his sandwich into his mouth. "Did you and your dad talk very often?"

"Yes, as a matter of fact, we did. Look—"

"Didn't it bother him that you preferred Oregon over Montana?"

"Of course it didn't bother him. Why should it? Listen—"

"Tell me about your home. Do you live near the coast?"

Internally Cass was seething. He kept interrupting her, deliberately avoiding conversation about that option.

"I live *on* the coast. My house is on a cliff overlooking the ocean. Gard—"

"That sounds terrific. Bet you have a great view."

Her patience came to an abrupt end. "You are without a doubt the most irritating person I have ever known." Scrambling to her feet, she bent over to pick up the foil wrappers from the sandwiches. "You've ridden me around in circles all morning, and now you want to ride for another two hours to see a ridge that couldn't possibly be washed away from spring runoff, no matter how much damned snow piled up in the mountains during the winter."

"Now you're mad." Gard spoke in a hurt, disbelieving voice, as though she were the most unfair woman on the face of the earth. Or in Montana, at least.

Cass faced him, all but breathing fire. "If I were a man, I'd punch you right in the nose!" Then she whirled to go to her horse and get away from this infuriating person. She was all through being nice to him, option or no option.

Gard, still sitting, caught her by the ankles. Down she came, landing mostly on top of him. "You..." The names she shrieked at him were very unladylike and quite descriptive. "Let me go, you snake in the grass, you weasel, you..." Again the unladylike names rolled out of her mouth.

Neatly and with a minimum of exertion, Gard rolled them over so that he was on top. "You sure do have a mouth on you, Sassy Whitfield. I think it's time someone taught you better manners."

"And you think *you're* the man to do it?" Cass let out a screech so loud and piercing, Gard thought it probably echoed throughout the entire valley. But she didn't only screech, she started fighting to get away.

And the wrestling match began.

Three

Cass squirmed and pushed and shoved. "You cretin!" She was wiry and quick, but so was Gard, and his strength was so superior he soon had her hands locked above her head while the weight of his body held her down.

What really infuriated her was that he thought rolling around on the ground like this was funny. Throughout their tussle she'd heard the low, sexy chuckle deep in his throat, and when she was finally unable to move anything but her toes, he grinned at her.

"You savage," she said, venting her wrath through clenched teeth. "Force is probably the only way you can get a woman on her back." He laughed as though she had said something hysterically funny. "Egotistical jerk." Cassandra turned her eyes to avoid his. No one she'd ever known had eyes as blue as Gard's. Right now they were brimming with amusement and she didn't want to see it.

He dipped his head slightly, bringing their faces closer.

"There are three things I'd like to do to you, Sassy Whitfield," he whispered. "Want to know what they are?"

"I most certainly do not!"

"Make that four, and I don't believe you don't want to know. In fact, I think you're dying to know, so I'm going to be kind and tell you. First, I'd like to turn you over my knee and paddle your sweet little behind. I think you've had it all your way for so long, you don't know how to deal with a man who doesn't jump at your command."

Cass's gaze jerked around. "Of all the... Just try it, and I'll scratch the eyes right out of your arrogant head!"

Gard laughed softly. "Second, I'd like to kiss you until you're limp all over and begging for more."

"Hell will freeze over before I ever beg *you* for anything," she sputtered.

"Third, once you're begging and whimpering, I'd like to make love to you. The right kind of love, Sassy, sensual and slow."

She had no cutting retort for that one. Being held down like this was humiliating, and so were his crude fantasies.

"The fourth thing I want from you is friendship," Gard said quietly.

"Yeah, right," she drawled, disdain all over her face. "Why did I ever think you and I could conduct business like two normal people? You're not the least bit normal."

"Oh, I'm pretty normal, honey. Can't you tell?"

What she could tell was that he was enormously aroused and not a bit averse to letting her know. It was a frustrating moment for Cass. Lying beneath him, feeling every contour of his body pressing into hers, her own hormones were beginning to misbehave.

"If friendship is what you want between us, you're going at it in a mighty strange way," she said sharply, denying the throbbing that had started at intimate points of her body. "Tripping me was abominable. So is holding me down this way. Don't you have any scruples at all?"

"Since paddling your behind would probably cause a ruckus we might never get over, how about going with the second item on my list and kissing each other senseless?"

She turned her gaze to give him a murderous look. He was having entirely too much fun at her expense. "You're already minus the sense God gave that tree over there. Let go of my hands!"

"So you can scratch out my eyes? That's what you said, honey, that you'd scratch the eyes right out of my arrogant head."

"This conversation is over. Let me up!"

"Not until you kiss me."

Cass gulped. The silky tone in his teasing voice was much too reminiscent of that night at the dunes. "You don't have the morals of an alley cat. I see it all now. This is the only reason you put on that big act of needing to inspect Whitfield land before making that decision, you...you..."

"Don't start with the name-calling again, Sassy, or I swear I'll hold you here for the rest of the day."

"You always were a damned bully," she said, fuming.

"I was never a bully and you know it. I did a lot of things I wish I hadn't, but bullying people wasn't one of them. If anything, I was too easygoing. I picked the wrong friends, or they picked me. Anyway, there was always someone around wanting to party, and I fully admit to acting like a jackass in my younger days."

"You're *still* acting like a jackass. Gard, this has gone far enough. Let me up!"

"After you kiss me."

"I am not going to kiss you!"

"Then how about just lying still and letting me kiss you?"

"Could I stop you?" she said angrily. Could she stop him from doing anything he wanted? Her face flamed at the thought. He wouldn't dare do more than kiss her, would he?

Gard brought his head down until his lips were almost touching hers. "You won't let yourself like me, and I want to know why."

"What you're doing right now is reason enough, don't you think?"

"I'm talking about before today. The afternoon you walked into that room at the Plantation, you were all bristled up like a little porcupine."

"That's a lie." She could feel his breath on her mouth and smell his after-shave, and worse, much worse, she was unable to ignore the blatant evidence of his manhood pressing into her abdomen. She wanted to stay angry, to remain furious and spiteful, but a languor was spreading throughout her body.

His gaze flicked over her face, feature by feature. His hold on her relaxed. She could easily elude him now if she wanted to. "You are a seriously beautiful woman, Cassandra Whitfield." Elation darted through him; she hadn't moved an inch. He placed his mouth tenderly on hers, and at just about the same moment, he wedged his legs in between hers and adjusted his position so that his arousal was firmly resting against her most private and sensitive spot.

Cass's brain seemed to divide, one portion suddenly aching with passion and the other trying desperately to cling to common sense. It would be so easy to get carried away, to just let go and kiss him back. He had succeeded in making her want him, in stirring up all of the eroticism she possessed, and the commonsense portion of herself was losing ground. His lips felt delectably sensual on hers, warm and tender, demanding and giving, all at the same time. Instead of feeling the substantial weight of his body, she felt its remarkable composition, his chest, his thighs, and most disturbing of all, his sex subtly moving against hers.

She was getting sweaty and weak, and her mouth had become yielding and soft under his, molding at his direction, opening for his tongue.

"Sassy," he whispered huskily.

Oh, God, she thought. She couldn't let this happen again, not when their first time had meant so little to him he had no memory of it. Her wounds from that episode had gone so deep she still felt them. Rebel Sterling wasn't the man for her to be fooling around with, however persuasive were his kisses and hard body.

With her hands freed, she laid them on either side of his head and pushed. Their mouths separated, and he looked at her with surprise in his eyes. Cass could almost see the protests lining up in his head, so she spoke first, hoarsely but fiercely. "Are you planning to take advantage of me again?"

Gard froze, his expression, his hands, his body, every inch of him. "What did you say?"

Already she wished she hadn't said it. It wasn't the truth, not the whole truth, and she could see what her accusation had done to him.

But neither could she take back the question. "I think you heard me."

"All right, I heard you, but why did you say something like that?" His voice was controlled only through intense effort. He'd taken advantage of her? When? Where? As the questions mounted in his mind, he could feel all traces of desire deserting his system.

But then a horrifying thought struck him: was it true? Was that why Cassandra had been so distant and unfriendly? Was that the event nagging at his flawed memory? Had he forced her into something sexual?

Abruptly he rolled away from her, ending up on his back, his face tense, his eyes shadowed with confusion. Cass sat up slowly, almost afraid to look at him. She never should have said such a thing. He hadn't taken advantage of her; he'd just made giving in to his charm seem natural and sensible, and while it had felt perfectly natural at the time, it certainly hadn't been sensible.

She sent him a quick, uneasy glance, wondering how to undo the damage she had just inflicted without getting into a detailed discussion of that night and its painful aftermath. There were some things she would never be able to tell him, such as the nights of crying herself to sleep because she'd seen him at some point of that day and he hadn't noticed her. Certainly he had never called or come to the house to see her. It was as though that night at the dunes had happened only in her own mind, and she'd been so hurt by his avoidance that nothing else in life held any meaning.

That was when she had made the decision to leave Montana. Her parents agreed on the further education she'd chosen, a small, well-respected art school in San Francisco, and she had packed and left, praying that time and distance would allow her to forget Gard Sterling.

She pushed herself to her feet and brushed off the seat of her jeans. "I'm sorry I said that."

Gard sat up. Something hurt in his stomach. Not a pain, exactly, more like a tearing, ripping sensation. He spoke raggedly. "Is it true?"

"I'd rather not talk about it." Nervous and trying not to show it, Cass started for her horse.

Gard jumped to his feet and rushed after her. He grabbed her by the arm, and not gently, either. *"Is it true?"*

She tried to wrench her arm free. "I *said* I don't want to talk about it!"

Gard's eyes were blazing. "That's just too damned bad! You're not leaving until you explain yourself. What you said is either a stupefying, deplorable fact or the most despicable lie I've ever heard. Now, which is it?"

Her own anger was rising. "What's wrong with your own memory? Don't you remember what you did years ago? How you behaved? Was the world really your oyster, or did you merely think it was? You were drunk or well on your way most of the time, and why anyone—including your father—put up with your selfishness escapes me completely."

"List every fault I ever had if it makes you feel superior, Cassandra, but don't try to evade the subject you introduced. Did I force you into something?" He winced at the question. Never in his wildest dreams could he have put himself in that scenario. Yes, there'd been many women, but what he remembered of them was willingness, eagerness, cooperation, participation.

Cass's face was flushed. "I've said all I'm going to say about it, so you may as well stop throwing your weight around. Just what makes you think you can manhandle me the way you've done today? You're still doing it!"

What he was doing was maintaining a tight grasp on her arm, though not with anything sexual in mind. She had struck a blow he wouldn't easily forget, and he had to know if there was any truth to it. His teeth clenched. "Give me a straight answer, damn you. Did I ever force you to have sex with me?"

She looked away from the turmoil in his eyes. "There are different kinds of force," she said stiffly.

Gard took her chin with his free hand and turned her head to face him. "So, we did have sex? When did it happen? Where? And what kind of force did I allegedly use to seduce you? Did I hold you down and rip off your clothes?"

Her lips pursed. "Not exactly." She had never wanted to have this conversation. Why in God's name hadn't she kept her big mouth shut?

"But I did get you out of your clothes. Where were we when this supposedly took place?"

If she didn't get away from him, he was going to pull every tiny detail out of her about that night. She gathered what strength she could and looked him right in the eyes. "I'm telling you to let go of my arm this instant. This conversation is over, and you can stew about it for the rest of your life for all I care."

His eyes had grown hard. "Do you care about that option?"

Her eyes hardened, also. "Are you going to try and blackmail me into talking about the past? Forget that idea, Gard. Frankly, after today I don't give a damn if you ever make that decision."

"I'll stop you from selling."

"That doesn't surprise me. You never were a decent person, and you'll probably still be a coldhearted, selfish S.O.B. on the day you die. Now, let me go!" This time when Cass pulled against his hand, he loosened his hold on her arm and let her move away. "Thank you," she said sarcastically.

His expression grim, Gard stood there and watched her walk to her horse. She mounted. He yelled as she rode away. "Have a good day, Cassandra. You sure as hell made mine!"

Internally Cass winced, though she kept going. How could those words have come out of her mouth? She had never used the word *force* in any description of that night at the dunes. Had it been lurking in the far recesses of her mind all this time?

She bit her lip, frowning at the ground ahead of her. Remembering Gard's words—that it was *either a stupefying, deplorable fact or the most despicable lie*—caused remorse to burn like acid in her stomach. If she had wanted to finally talk to Gard about that night, why had she chosen to blurt out a ghastly accusation instead of merely...

Merely what? Hadn't his faulty memory been gnawing at her? How dare he make love to a woman and then simply put it out of his mind, as though it had been of no more import than... than crossing a street? Why should she be feeling guilty and as though she had committed some unpardonable sin?

Tears were suddenly blurring Cass's vision. She should have known that Gard would not only prove uncooperative regarding the contract, but that he would do something else to make her miserable. She should have left the matter in the hands of their lawyers, as she had initially intended.

Well, that was the way it would be from now on. There was not going to be any more personal contact between her and Gard Sterling, not if she had to desert the ranch and Montana to accomplish it.

* * *

Gard stared after Cassandra through narrowed, disturbed eyes as she and her horse got smaller in the distance. He had never been so shaken before in his life. How many times would some idiotic thing he'd done years ago suddenly flash into his mind and bring him to his knees with regret?

But nothing from his wild and hedonistic youth had hit him the way Cassandra's allegation had. Was there any truth to it? She had backed down slightly, but even though he couldn't remember the event, he suspected—very strongly—that they had made love, or rather, had sex—under some circumstance.

How old had she been when she left the valley? Gard had to think hard to come up with an approximate age. Seventeen or eighteen...somewhere along there. Damn! He slammed his fist into his other palm. A kid, and he'd made love to her and couldn't even remember doing it.

But *she* remembered. Remembered so well that she could barely speak civilly to him.

Slowly Gard walked to where he'd tied his horse. The feelings he'd developed rose up to mock him. Certainly Cassandra had become interesting to him at their first meeting. He'd seen and appreciated her pretty face and remarkable figure. More, he'd felt that intangible chemistry that made one woman stand out from others.

Now there wasn't a snowball's chance in hell of anything important occurring between them. He'd behaved like an adolescent, assuming that she was as attracted to him as he was to her. Kissing her...pressuring her...talking like a fool about paddling her behind and making love...thinking that her protests were merely coyness and flirting.

His ego had been badly damaged today. Cassandra was no slouch in the hit-'em-where-it-hurts department, and he resented her cruel method of letting him know where they stood with each other. She could have used a little tact, couldn't she?

But then, he hadn't been exactly tactful, either. Meeting Cassandra at the Plantation that day had been like meeting her for the first time ever. The girl he remembered—vaguely, to be sure—had barely been recognizable in the stylish, sophisticated woman who had walked into that banquet room. He'd started off on the wrong foot with Cassandra simply because he hadn't had a clue about her true state of mind.

Tight-lipped and tense, Gard mounted his horse and began the ride home. To his *own* home. What did he do now? he thought dismally. They still had the contract to deal with, even though Cassandra had plainly and angrily stated that she didn't give a damn if he ever made a decision on that option.

Would she cool down and talk to him again? When should he try to find out? This evening? He could call and apologize, even though he couldn't remember what he'd be apologizing for. Maybe he should apologize for that, as well. *Cassandra, I'm sorry I can't remember making love to you.*

Gard winced. An apology of that sort was apt to earn him a behind full of buckshot, should he ever get near enough for her to haul out that shotgun she'd mentioned.

Admit it, Sterling. You've made one hell of a mess of things, and this is one time that an apology might do more harm than good.

But how did a man untangle this kind of chaotic muddle? Leaving the situation as it was now was unthinkable. Something had to be done. Cassandra thought the absolute worst of him, and that knowledge hurt like the very devil. He didn't *want* her thinking he was the same careless, pleasure-seeking, self-indulgent swinger he'd been fourteen years ago. The signs of his present calm and temperate lifestyle were completely evident, which she would have seen right away if she hadn't been so biased by the past.

On the other hand, he himself had negated those signs by behaving like a wet-behind-the-ears, horny kid. That was the crux of this thing, Gard thought uneasily. Neither of them were kids anymore, and for some god-awful reason their meeting had set off a sort of regression that had Cassandra despising him for something he obviously should have remembered, and him, in his ignorance, getting all silly and excited over a pretty face.

Gard got home without reaching a solution. One thing was for certain: the sparks between himself and Cassandra were real. The yielding softness of her lips wasn't only in his imagination. For a few seconds there on the ground, she had kissed him back. The pliancy of her body under his had felt too good to have been anything else. However determined she was to hate him—and he did believe that was the case—she was affected by him physically, just as she affected him.

Grim-lipped, Gard unsaddled his horse and tended the animal. Maybe, he thought, this thing with Cassandra was a matter of which of them had the most determination. In any case, it wasn't over. He still wanted a full explanation of what he'd supposedly done to get her clothes off, and yes, it would be mighty interesting to hear what *she* had been doing while he was undressing her. There was a whole lot more to the story than the meager glimpses Cassandra had allowed him today, and damn his own defective memory for denying him the facts of the event.

He stopped with a can of oats in his hand to swear an oath. If it took the rest of his life to accomplish it, he was going to hear it all.

Four

Seated at the desk in the study that evening, Cass talked on the phone with her attorney. "I've tried everything, Peter, and he simply will not give me an answer. Do you have any further suggestions?"

"It's the lack of a specific time limit in the contract that's permitting Sterling's procrastination, Cass."

"I realize that, but reasonable time, as cited in the contract, shouldn't allow him to drag this out indefinitely. What does 'reasonable time' mean to you?"

Peter cleared his throat. "Well... off the top of my head I would think a few months should be enough time for a person to make a decision of this nature. But a personal opinion doesn't count for much, Cassandra."

"A judge's opinion might."

"Do you wish to initiate a lawsuit?"

Cass hesitated. "I... don't know. What do you think?" She was still so upset about what she'd said to Gard, it was difficult to concentrate on anything else.

"Well . . . since you asked, I feel that you should give him more time. He's had three months. Give him another three. Then, if he's still dragging his heels, we can go to court and test the legality of that contract."

"Three months." Cass sighed. Francis would not wait for another three months, so she might as well kiss that opportunity goodbye. And neither could she hang around here for three more months. She would go home and rely on the people working on the ranch to take care of it. She could stay in touch by telephone, and even make a trip or two back to Montana to check its care for herself.

"Well, thanks for the advice, Peter. It isn't what I'd hoped to hear, but I'm sure you know more about these things than I do." Her voice was dull and rather lifeless.

"Call anytime, Cass."

"Thanks, I will. Bye."

Cass remained seated at the desk, staring into space. But it wasn't only Peter's advice that had her buried in a blue funk, it was her own faux pas today with Gard. He hadn't forced her into anything, unless sweet talk, hot kisses and masculine persuasion could be construed as force. But he certainly hadn't ripped off her clothes, as he'd sarcastically suggested. In fact, he'd been rougher and more physical with her today than he'd been that night at the dunes.

Going back in time, Cass sat back and closed her eyes. She had driven home from the dunes that night in an ecstatic, romantic daze: Gard Sterling had finally noticed her as a woman. She thought she was in love, and though Gard hadn't said he loved her, she was certain he did.

It was a few days later, when surprised that he hadn't yet called or come by the ranch, she had stood on the street in town and watched him ride past on his motorcycle with barely a nod of recognition in her direction. She had called out, "Gard!" But he either hadn't heard her or had deliberately ignored the summons, because he'd kept on going.

That was when the pain began, the humiliation. She'd tried talking herself out of thinking the worst, making excuses for his rudeness. But it happened again... and then again... and finally she knew in her badly bruised soul that Gard Sterling was never going to do more than say a casual hello to her. That night had meant nothing to him. She was just another girl to Rebel Sterling, just another easy mark.

At the desk, Cass shivered as though struck by a sudden chill. Whatever Gard's sins of the past, he wasn't guilty of force, and today she had led him to believe otherwise. Not intentionally. Why those words had come out of her mouth, she would never know. Maybe they'd been dredged up from old resentments, or more likely, because he was making her want him again.

Whatever, the damage was done and Cass couldn't think of any way to undo it short of an explanation of that long-ago night. But how in God's name could she force herself to initiate such a conversation? She had never talked about that night with anyone, and the thought of doing so with Gard made her stomach roll threateningly.

She got up to pace the study, curling her arms around herself, a deep furrow of remorse between her eyes. Letting him worry about it—even though she'd told him he could stew for the rest of his life and she wouldn't care—went deeply against her grain. Normally she was a friendly, generous and considerate woman. Her friends in Oregon thought so, she knew. Only with Gard was she tense and waspish.

"What should I do?" she whispered. It was a question she took to bed with her an hour later and kept her restless throughout the night.

Gard was stunned—there was no other word for it—to open his front door around eight the following evening and see Cassandra Whitfield standing on his porch. She was wearing a blue denim skirt and a white blouse, casual clothing, and though she looked pretty and feminine, as usual, her face bore a harried expression. In fact, her eyes wouldn't quite meet his. "May we talk for a few minutes?" she asked.

He didn't know what to make of this visit. After yesterday he would have sworn on his parents' memory that Cassandra Whitfield would never step foot on Sterling land. "Uh, sure. Come on in."

The Sterling house had a wide front porch with several chairs. "Let's sit out here," she said quietly.

"If you prefer." Closing the door behind him, Gard gestured at the chairs. "Take your pick."

"Thank you." Cass sat down, but Gard leaned his hips against the porch railing and leveled a hard look on her. Her hair was down, kissing her shoulders, and her pretty face and femaleness raised his ire.

Cass took a breath. "I want to say something, but before I get to it, I think you should know that I'm going home. My lawyer suggested giving you another three months to make your decision, and I've decided to abide by his advice."

Gard pondered the information, wondering if he would be in a better fiscal condition in three months. But that contract just wasn't very important anymore. He could be kind and tell her straight out that he didn't have the money to buy her property, which would put an end to her concerns regarding that buy/sell option. But he really didn't feel like being kind to Cassandra Whitfield right now. Since yesterday's altercation, in fact, Gard's mood had been as black as coal dust.

"So, you're leaving," he said coldly. "You probably won't mind my saying that I'm glad."

"Why should you care one way or the other?" she snapped, startled to defensiveness by his rude remark.

Gard leaned forward slightly. "After what you accused me of yesterday, you have to ask?"

Cass straightened her shoulders. "That's what I came to talk about." She looked around. "Are we alone? Is there anyone nearby to hear us talking?"

"There are people on the ranch. I suppose someone could overhear us. Why? Are you and I going to have a personal conversation, Sassy Cassie?"

"Please don't use that ludicrous nickname, and if your end of this conversation is going to be underlaid with sarcasm, we may as well forget it." Cass got to her feet. "I shouldn't have come here."

Gard hesitated only a moment. "Come on. We'll take a walk, and I guarantee no one will hear anything we say." What was she planning to do, reinforce yesterday's accusation? If that was the case, he'd just as soon not have anyone hearing it, either.

They left the porch. Gard chose the direction, heading toward an open field, and Cass walked with him. It was a glorious evening, unusually warm and mellow. A frisson of nervous energy darted up Cass's spine. There was the same kind of velvety warmth in the air this evening as there'd been on that long-ago night at the sand dunes, she realized.

When they were well away from the buildings and obviously alone, she stopped walking, anxious to get this over with. Gard halted his steps and looked at her. "Go ahead and say it." He'd spoken gruffly, belligerently.

Cass looked at him with some surprise. "Do you know what I came to say?"

"I have a pretty good idea."

"Then you remember?"

"Remember what?"

Disappointed, she released the breath she'd been holding. "You don't have the vaguest idea of why I'm here, so do me a favor, okay? Just listen and then let me leave without a deluge of questions." She cleared her throat and forced herself to look him in the eye. "You didn't force me, and I'm sick to my stomach that I said you did. That's what I came to say, and I hope it makes you feel better. I know it bothered you..."

"Bothered me!" Laughing humorlessly, Gard ran the fingers of both hands through his hair. "A mosquito taking his supper out of my hide bothers me, baby. A flat tire on my pickup bothers me." He put his face right in Cass's. "A letter from the IRS *bothers* me. What you said yesterday..." He was suddenly so furious that he had to back away from her. After a moment he felt a little calmer, though the burning in his gut was still glaringly present. "Why did you say it if it isn't true?"

"I don't intend to stand here and answer a barrage of questions. I apologized and that's the end of it." Cass turned to go. "I'll contact you in three months, or my lawyer will, unless you make up your mind before that and contact one of us. Goodbye."

Gard stared after her. Cassandra Whitfield's gall was stupefying. She thought she could come to his own home, apologize for accusing him of something he found morally degrading, and then walk away as though the entire incident had vanished into thin air.

"Just a minute," he said brusquely, taking long strides to catch up with her. "This conversation isn't over."

Cass was nearly to her car, and she kept going until her fingers were curled around the door handle. "This conversation *is* over," she rebutted. "I did what I came to do and now I'm leaving." She opened the door of her car and slid into the driver's seat.

Gard saw red, and wanted to pull her out of that car and shake her until her teeth rattled. For some reason she had put the keys into a pocket of her skirt instead of leaving them in the ignition, and it was taking her a moment to fish them out.

Without hesitating a second, Gard loped around the back of the car, opened the passenger door and got in. Cass's head jerked around, her eyes wide and startled. "Just what do you think you're doing now?"

"You might think this conversation is over, sweetheart, but *I* think it just got started."

"Get out, Gard," she said menacingly.

"I'm not getting out until you talk to me."

Cass's anger was nearing the explosive stage. "Your arrogance is astounding! Get your butt out of my car!"

With his eyes hard as sapphires, Gard turned in the seat to face her. "What happened between us? Where did it happen? When?"

"I'm telling you nothing! Dig into your own damned memory if you want more information!" Cass began fumbling with the keys and the ignition, though her hand was shaking so badly she couldn't make the connection. "Damn you!" she cried. "I worried all night about what I said. I didn't have to come over here and apologize, and now you're making it very clear that I shouldn't have been one bit concerned about your feelings."

"It won't kill you to give me a few answers. You worried all night? What the hell do you think I did? No woman's ever accused me of force before, and—"

"And maybe someone should have! You had the worst reputation of anyone in the area, and you know it was well deserved."

"Yes, it was. I don't try to kid myself about the kind of person I was in those days. Cassie..." The steel in his eyes relented a little. "When did we make love?"

Closing her eyes, she heaved a heavy sigh. "You're going to keep right on badgering me, aren't you?"

"Wouldn't you, if the shoe were on the other foot?"

It was a startling thought, but not so startling that she was ready to divulge her one and only secret. From their convoluted conversations, he had deduced that they had made love at some point in time, obviously in the distant past. And no, she couldn't blame him for being curious.

But she had already told him too much. "We didn't make love," she said frostily. "We had sex. There is a difference, you know. Now, please get out of my car and let me leave."

"Why are you doing this?"

Cass's eyes flashed to his. "Hasn't it occurred to you that some things are too painful to talk about? Why do you need to hear every little detail? It was a long time ago and has no bearing on the present."

Silently, broodingly, Gard stared at her. "Sounds to me like it has a lot of bearing on the present if you can't talk about it after fourteen years. Or was it longer than that? How old were you when it happened? How old was I?" He leaned closer to her. "Cassie, were we just youngsters fooling around, or were we older?"

"You were old enough to be drunk!" she retorted. Then she wearily rubbed her forehead with her fingertips, a rather defeated gesture. "You were drunk and I was stupid. It happened at the sand dunes. I hope that satisfies your curiosity, because it's my last word on the subject." This time she succeeded in inserting the right key into the ignition. "I'm going to leave." She started the engine. "Unless you intend going home with me, I suggest you get out."

Gard had been sitting very still. "I think I'm finally getting the picture," he said softly.

"Wonderful," Cass returned with heavy sarcasm.

"We ran into each other at the sand dunes, right? Or maybe I brought you out there on my motorcycle. It was probably a nice evening, like this one, warm and silky. We kissed, probably necked a little, and then things started happening. Yeah, that sounds pretty logical. Is it logical, Cassie? Is that what happened?"

"What happened was *not* logical," she replied stonily.

"But you cooperated, right? You wanted what I did."

Cass moaned. "Will you never stop?" She couldn't sit there and listen to his "logic" another second, and she turned off the engine and jumped out of the car.

Gard got out, too, frowning because she was marching down the driveway toward the highway. "Hey, where are you going?"

"Home!"

"You're going to walk? What about your car?"

She turned around and skipped backward, as though she couldn't stop moving for any reason. "Just shut the hell up,

Gard Sterling! Don't ever talk to me again, not about anything!'' Turning again, she began jogging.

Gard came around her car at a good clip. ''You little idiot,'' he mumbled. Cassandra leaving her car behind because he was sitting in it wasn't exactly a bright move. It was at least five miles from his house to hers and it was getting dark. With a put-upon sigh, he climbed into her car, started it, turned it around and began driving toward the highway.

He was alongside Cass in less than a minute. ''You're behaving like a spoiled brat,'' he yelled out the open window. She kept on jogging, never even glancing his way. ''Cassandra, this is ridiculous!''

Gard maintained her speed; she was on the left side of the driveway, he was on the right. It was half a mile from his house to the highway, and they were about halfway there. Disgustedly, Gard stepped on the gas and shot ahead of her. Then, at the highway, he braked to a stop, turned off the engine and got out to wait for her to catch up.

Leaning against the trunk of her car, he folded his arms across his chest and watched her getting closer in the fading light. When she saw him, she slowed down to a walk. In Oregon she jogged regularly, but she hadn't had much exercise for the three months she'd been in Montana and the run had winded her. Even if Gard and her car hadn't been there, she would have needed a moment to catch her breath.

''One question,'' Gard said darkly when she walked up. ''If I didn't force you, if you wanted what I did, why do you hate me for it?''

Hate him? Looking at him in the deepening dusk, she realized again that she had never hated him. His long, lanky body leaning against her car was unutterably appealing, and maybe that was what angered her the most, that she could still find him attractive and sexy after all the pain he had caused her.

But that was something he would never hear. He would never know how she had suffered over his silence, or that she had envisioned herself in love with him, or that she had nearly died of humiliation when his disregard became apparent.

Cass stood there in the twilight, attempting to devise an answer that would put an end to Gard's curiosity and her own anger. It had happened so long ago. For her own peace of mind it was time to scratch it off, to forget it.

"I don't hate you," she said evenly. "May I take my car and leave now?"

There was an emptiness in Gard, a sense of desolation. She had told him all she was going to about their misadventure at the sand dunes, and she was leaving Montana, probably for good. "Take your car," he said quietly. "But let me say something first. I'm sorry, Cass. I did so many things in those days I'm sorry for now. There were a lot of women—" Cass winced. "And today, in my memory, very few of them have faces. I never should have involved you in my..." He stopped for a moment. "I don't know what to call how I lived then. I'm not proud of it, and...I'm sorry."

An enormous lump had risen in Cass's throat during Gard's impassioned speech. Her voice came out sounding husky and emotional. "It's in the past. Let's just forget it."

"That's good advice...but I'm not sure I can do it." Gard moved away from her car. "About that option..."

Cass walked past him to the driver's side of the car. "I'm reconciled to waiting another three months, so take your time." Feeling wrung out, Cass got into the car and Gard didn't try to stop her. "Goodbye."

"Bye, Cassie," he said softly. He hated her driving out of his life, but that's what she was doing. He stood there until her taillights had vanished, then turned and started the half-mile hike back to the house.

Cass was driving with tears in her eyes. Maneuvering a tissue out of her purse with one hand, she wiped the tears dribbling down her cheeks, only to feel another stream of them. The tissue was soon soggy, and still the tears came.

She didn't want to go home and spend the remainder of the evening wiping away tears. Gard's emotional apology had torn her up, and she wasn't apt to recover from its effect for a while. Making a left turn from the highway, she headed for the sand dunes; it was as good a place as any to cry herself senseless.

Cass had always loved the hills of golden sand that rose from the valley floor in undulating waves, so divergent from the surrounding terrain. As a girl she had fantasized about the dunes. One of her youthful ideas was that a slight miscalculation by the Almighty had set the dunes down in Montana rather than in a desert, but mentioning that theory to her father had earned her a lecture of a religious nature. "It's merely the geology of the area," Ridge Whitfield had sternly stated.

Whatever magic had created the dunes amid grass and sage, prairie and mountains, they had always been a favorite haunt of Cass's. As a child she had often begged her parents to take her there, and she would run barefoot though the sand, up one hill, down another. When she got her driver's license and the use of an old Jeep of her father's, she drove herself to the dunes. Day or night, whenever she wanted to be alone, whenever she needed some quiet time to think over a problem, or to ponder life, to puzzle over her future, she would drive to the dunes.

But she hadn't gotten near the dunes in years. Her visits home since the completion of her education had been brief, and spent with her father. Her mother died while Cass was in her final year of school, and that trip home had been grievous and emotional.

Dad, do you want me to come home to stay so you won't be alone?

What were you planning to do, honey?

I've spent some time on the Oregon coast with friends, and... well, there's a big, old house for sale on a cliff overlooking the ocean that I'd love to own. It's badly run-down, so it's offered at a rock-bottom price. I've been thinking how I could fix it up. Dad, it has the most incredible windows facing the water. The light is perfect for my work. The top floor—there are three levels—would make a wonderful studio.

Ridge had told her with all sincerity that she must live her life in her own way. *If you want that house and want to live in Oregon, then that's what you should do, honey.* He'd given her the money to purchase the property. He had always been generous with her, but buying her that house had always held special meaning for Cass. *Well, why in heck wouldn't I buy it for you? You're my only daughter. Anything I have is yours for the asking, honey-girl.*

Cass had never doubted her father's love. He had not only given her financial support until her paintings began selling, he'd been morally supportive. *You're an artist, honey, and a darned good one. Stay with it. You'll succeed, mark my words.*

Those thoughts mingled with those concerning Gard as Cass parked her car and got out. It had grown completely dark, and once the headlights were turned off she had to rely on the stars and the moon to orient herself. With a handful of tissues, she left her car and climbed to the top of a dune, where she sat down to have that good cry.

Gard approached the ranch house, then stopped dead in his tracks. He didn't feel like going in and going to bed. The turmoil in his system wasn't going to make sleep come easily tonight, and he'd thought of what Cass had said—*It happened at the dunes*—all during his hike from the highway.

Cass's admission had awakened segments of Gard's memory, and he remembered taking a six-pack of beer and riding his Harley-Davidson out to the dunes every so often. Those had been the evenings when he hadn't wanted company. His hangouts—the pool hall and various taverns—were rarely without pals eager for a good time. But occasionally he'd wanted to be by himself, and he'd hop on the motorcycle and head for some out-of-the-way spot where no one would think to look for him. The dunes, he had discovered, were a great place to watch the moon rise or set, and he would sometimes sit in the sand sipping beer for hours on end.

Now, standing in his own yard, about halfway between the house and where his pickup was parked, he realized that a good many years had passed since his last visit to the dunes. Maybe something out there would further jog his memory. The subject might be closed for Cassandra, but questions were gnawing at him, one in particular: had he brought Cassandra to the dunes, or had they merely found themselves in the same place at the same time?

What was the whole story, dammit? Cassandra Whitfield had never been a possible girlfriend. She had been that much younger than himself that he'd never thought of her in that way. She was the girl on the next ranch, a pretty kid he remembered teasing and then laughing with because she was so quick on the comeback.

Reflecting on it all, Gard walked to his truck and got in. Driving to the highway, he wondered how in hell they had progressed from neighbors to lovers in one fell swoop. *Had* he used some sort of force? She had said there were all kinds of force, whatever that meant, so maybe he had pressured her into doing something she really hadn't wanted.

Angrily he slapped the steering wheel. Why couldn't he remember what Cassie did? Okay, so he'd been drinking. According to her, anyway. *You were drunk and I was stupid.* Obviously she viewed their encounter with extreme distaste. If only he knew exactly *when* it had happened. He'd seen her every so often during the summer before she'd gone off to college—he at least remembered that—and she'd never given any sign that anything intimate had occurred between them.

The road to the dunes was a series of curves and swells. Gard drove at an easy speed, his mind on Cassandra and the past. She'd said she didn't hate him, but her antagonism contradicted that statement. And yet, when he'd kissed her, he'd felt the warmth of her lips against his. She was ambivalent where he was concerned, he suddenly realized with a narrowing of his eyes. Ambivalent and unhappy about it.

Well, he wasn't happy about it, either. It seemed damned unfair that he had finally met a woman who could become important to him, and she was carrying around an old memory that obstructed a serious relationship for them.

The dunes came into view. There was one more sharp curve in the road to reach them. Gard took it slow and easy, and then he spotted the car. All the way out there, he had seen no other vehicles, not a soul, and another visitor to the dunes this night was disruptive to his state of mind.

Until he got closer and saw whose car it was. He could hardly believe his eyes. Instead of going home, Cassandra had come here.

Gard parked the truck and turned off the engine. The ensuing silence was almost eerie. Getting out, he ambled over to Cassandra's car and peered in.

Then he stood there frowning and looking at the dunes, hoping to catch sight of her. It disturbed him that she had come out here alone after dark.

But wasn't it strange that he had also decided to drive out here tonight?

Five

Cass heard a vehicle coming. The parking area wasn't visible from her particular patch of sand and, thinking that she should check on whoever else had decided to visit the dunes tonight, she got up and slogged along to a spot with a view—such as it was in the dark—of her car and the newcomer's. It was a pickup truck. She squinted at the pickup, then her entire body tensed in recognition. How *dare* Gard follow her?

Her ricocheting emotions still hadn't completely settled down. Regardless, her common sense kicked in with a conclusion that Gard couldn't have followed her as too much time had elapsed between her arrival and his. So this was one of those unexplainable, unnerving coincidences: instead of going home, as she had announced to Gard, she had come to the dunes. Instead of Gard going to bed or a hundred other activities he could have chosen, he had come to the dunes.

But one would think, she thought peevishly, that upon seeing her car—there was no way he could miss it—he would have the tact to turn around and leave. Instead, she saw by peering into the dark that he was walking over to her car to see if she was in it!

Standing very still, she watched him look up at the dunes, obviously checking their shadowy dips and moonlit peaks in an attempt to spot her location. The prospect of another question-and-answer session with Gard was demoralizing, and yet the beating of her pulse signified a personal awareness of where they were, at the dunes where it had all begun. She knew intuitively that he was going to do his utmost to find her. She could call out and make it easy for him, or she could let him trudge through the sand and do his own looking. There was always the possibility, of course, of him missing her completely in the dark, which undoubtedly would be best.

But best or not, was that what she preferred? What fate had directed their paths tonight?

Gathering her skirt around her legs, Cass sat down. Since her tears had stopped flowing she had been doing some heavy-duty thinking. There was the lost opportunity to buy into the Deering Gallery to lament, of course, and she had to call Francis with the bad news. At least, Cass considered it bad news. According to Francis, there were buyers waiting in the wings, so at least *she* wasn't going to be financially disappointed.

But there were other things for Cass to think about. Unfinished canvases in her studio awaited her return to Oregon, and as always, regardless of how many other activities and thought-provoking subjects demanded her time, new ideas and various techniques for her work were forever percolating in the back of her mind. Her decision to go home for the additional three months she'd given Gard was wise and sensible, if for no other reason than to get back to work.

But Gard's emotional apology this evening had created a disruptive wave in her already confused system. He seemed to be very different from the wild, rebellious young man he'd been fourteen years ago, although it had taken her some time to face that fact. Whatever had caused the change was a complete mystery, but these days he drove a pickup instead of a motorcycle. Now he drank ice tea or coffee rather than beer or hard liquor. She'd seen enough of the Sterling ranch this evening to know that he was operating it as his father had. Today the name "Rebel" didn't fit; he appeared to be, as he had told her several times, a solid citizen.

But was it really possible for a man, for anyone, to change so drastically? Beneath his much calmer exterior, deep down where it counted, weren't there still some remnants of the defiance that Gard had constantly flaunted? Wouldn't a woman be unutterably foolish to fall for the same man twice, merely because he *seemed* to have finally grown up?

"Cassandra?"

She heard him coming and remained perfectly still, her gaze focused straight ahead on the waves of sand glistening in the moonlight. Even though she knew differently, she asked, "Did you follow me out here?"

"I had no idea you were coming here until I saw your car. I thought you were going home." Gard paused. "Do you believe me?"

Cass slowly turned and tilted her head to look at him. "Yes."

"Mind if I sit down?"

There were acres of sand, all public land, and his polite request nearly made her smile. "Do what you want, Gard. I suspect you usually do." He sank to the sand beside her, leaving plenty of space between them.

She took note of the width of sand between their bodies and experienced a prickling of her skin, positive that she could feel his warmth drifting toward her across that seemingly unbreachable span. "Do you come here often?" she questioned.

"I haven't been here in years." She was again looking across the dunes, and she heard him sigh. "I was really surprised to see your car. Aren't you afraid to be out here alone?"

Now she did smile. "Afraid of what?"

"Of someone coming along."

Her head turned to look at him. "Someone *did* come along. Should I be afraid?"

"Cassandra, I'm talking about strangers. There are some real wackos wandering the streets."

"Sorry to burst your protective bubble, but the dunes are completely devoid of wackos tonight." She added after a moment, "Other than you and I." She gave him a sidelong glance. "You're kind of wacky, and I guess I am, too."

Gard grinned, his first since yesterday. "Maybe so." His expression sobered. There were so many questions in his brain. *Did we simply run into each other out here when it happened, or did I bring you? Did we undress? Where did we do it, on the sand, in a car? If I was too drunk to remember it the next day, how was I able to perform?*

But he already knew the answer to that last question. Drinking might have made his brain too dizzy to speak clearly in his misspent youth, but booze had never affected him below his belt. Besides, Cass had said it straight out: they'd had sex.

Had he done a good job? Had he satisfied her?

He turned to look at her, suspecting that if he even got near that subject she'd get up and leave. Lord, she was pretty in the moonlight. Her hair looked like spun gold, and the features of her face, shadowed as they were, seemed to contain the mystery of the ages.

"Are you really leaving Montana?" he asked quietly.

Cass nodded. "I need to get back to work."

"Are you earning a living from your paintings?"

"I am now. Dad supported me for a long time. If it hadn't been for him, I wouldn't have had the financial means to stay with it long enough to accomplish anything." Ridge's death was still with her, still an underlying sorrow. It was going to take much longer than the three months she'd been in Montana to get over the shock of losing her father. But there was also pride in her voice, pride that Ridge had had such faith in her talent that he had insisted she pursue it.

"So you're a bona fide artist. I don't know any other artists, unless you count Sonny Fielding and his chain saw sculptures. Have you seen his work?"

"I don't remember the name. Maybe he moved here after I left."

"Possibly."

"I'm no judge of sculpture, anyway. Sonny Fielding could be a genius and I wouldn't know it."

Gard chuckled. "I think we can safely say he's not a genius. He does animals, and it's hard to tell what it is you're looking at, a rhinoceros or a bear."

Cass smiled. "Oh. Well . . . at least he's doing something he enjoys." It occurred to Cass that they were talking like any two normal people, and she wondered if being nice to Gard wasn't being traitorous to herself. But she'd been so torn up and now she wasn't. That good cry had helped, but Gard sitting with her on this hill of sand, beneath a star-studded sky, was strangely comforting.

Damn, she thought dismally. Did she even know her own mind anymore? For fourteen years she had resented this man and what he'd done, and now she found his presence comforting? Maybe she was even wackier than she'd admitted to being a few minutes ago.

She felt his eyes on her and finally looked back. "What?"

Gard spoke softly. "I was wishing we had met for the first time this summer. No past, no hard feelings, no . . ."

"Don't waste your time wishing for the impossible." But she was still gazing into his eyes, which looked blacker than the night sky and seemed to be saying something to her. It was disturbing to think she might never have gotten over that old crush, however badly he had hurt her. But she felt his presence deep inside of herself, his nearness, and easily she could imagine herself as seventeen again and gaga-eyed over the wildest, rowdiest boy in the county.

Except, of course, Gard hadn't been a boy; he'd been a man in his twenties.

"Don't look at me like that," she said, trying to sound strong and in control.

"How am I looking at you, Cassandra?" he asked softly.

"You know how."

"All right, we both know how. Does my interest offend you?" Inwardly he flinched. His question had given her an opening to lambaste the hell out of him, and not only for his misdeeds from the past. But twice since her return he had grabbed her and kissed her, and neither time had she invited any such attentions.

Cass breathed in, slowly, and then out, also slowly. "Why are you interested?"

It wasn't the reply he'd expected, and a gladness that she hadn't responded with some cutting remark warmed him. "Why is any man interested in one particular woman? For want of a better word, call it chemistry, Cassie. You're a beautiful woman, and I feel you in here." He tapped his chest. She was still looking at him, still sitting next to him, but dare he interpret her mood as receptive?

That thought had no more than formed in his mind when she abruptly broke eye contact by turning her head. "You might feel some chemistry between us, but I don't."

Her words felt like a blow and sounded like a lie. "Know what I think, Cassie? I think you *are* afraid of me. I think you feel our chemistry just as strongly as I do, only you won't let go of the past and admit it."

She scoffed. "That's absurd, but think what you want. It's really quite immaterial to me."

They fell silent, each involved in their own thoughts. Gard's took a surprising direction. "How come you never married?"

Her head jerked around. "That's none of your business. But since you mentioned it, how come *you* never married?"

Gard laughed softly. "Your personal life is none of my business, but mine is open for discussion? Well, I have none of your compunctions about talking about myself, Cassie. I suppose I never got married because the right woman never came along."

"I never took you for a romantic," she said somewhat sarcastically. "It's more likely that there were always so many women, you couldn't settle for only one."

"You're still thinking in the past, Cassandra."

"Don't expect me to believe there aren't any women in your life these days, Gard."

A pause ensued. Gard spoke first. "You're right. There is one."

"*Only* one?" His admission shouldn't hurt, but it did. Of course there was a woman. Gard Sterling would never live without sex for long.

"Only one," he affirmed. "Would you like to know her name?"

"God, no." Tears were threatening again, and if she cried now, Cass would despise herself for the rest of her days. "Why on earth would I want to know her name?"

Gard took her chin and turned her face to look into her eyes. "Her name is Cassandra Whitfield."

She froze. "Don't..."

But he did, and his lips on hers were as soft as rose petals, a gentle kiss that conveyed tender feelings. She let it happen. She sat there unmoving and let his lips play with hers, and in the bottom of her stomach she felt the birth of desire.

Her acceptance of his kiss made Gard's head spin. His hands had been idle, but now he raised them from the sand and took her by her shoulders, turning her toward him. Her lips parted for another kiss, and he could see that her eyes were closed. "Cassie," he whispered before uniting their mouths again.

Her lips moved under his, molding to his. He became bolder and slowly slid his tongue into her mouth. Her soft moan raised his blood pressure, and he deepened the kiss, opening his mouth to possess hers completely. The hunger of desire began controlling his movements. She was so womanly and soft, and she smelled so good, of something faintly flowery.

Cass wasn't unaware of what was happening, but she didn't have the strength of will to stop it. Other men's kisses paled in comparison to Gard's. No other man had ever made her feel what Gard did, that rush of feverish desire, that melting of bone and tissue, the overwhelming need that demanded another kiss, another caress.

He laid her back and leaned over her, kissing her mouth, her eyes, her cheeks and forehead. Then his lips glided down to her throat, and he felt her arms lift to clasp around his neck. "Oh, Cassie," he mumbled hoarsely. His mouth covered hers with breathtaking impact. One kiss flowed into another, and then another. Cass tried to think, to get a grasp on reality, but Gard felt so good, so right. Lying with him on the sand felt right, the warm, sensual night felt right.

Gard's hands were no longer idle. One glided slowly from her shoulder, down over her breast to her waist, and then down farther to her thigh. Every inch of her being touched by his fingers and palm tingled as though suddenly bursting to life. Her own hands explored the crisp hair at the back of his head, and his neck, his shoulders. The heat of his body mingled with hers, and the night temperature no longer seemed warm and balmy but rather hot and steamy.

She wanted him, wanted all of him. Kisses and caresses through clothing were not enough. Moaning, she arched into his body, and then moaned again at the wild excitement of fitting her curves to his.

"Cassie... baby," Gard whispered thickly. Her response was intoxicating, inflaming. Altering his position just enough to make room for his hand to squeeze between them, he pulled the bottom of her blouse free from the waistband of her skirt. He took her sigh into his own mouth when he pushed her bra up and out of the way and cupped her bare breast.

But then a small dose of reality managed to intrude—the sand. He could feel grains of it between his palm and her breast and knew they couldn't make full and complete love without something to lie on.

Gard blinked as a flash of memory tore through his brain: a blanket! He and a woman had made love on a blanket out here a long time ago. But which woman? Raising his head slightly, he studied Cassie's face in the moonlight. He wanted to ask if they had used a blanket their first time together, but fear that any sort of reference to that event would destroy Cassie's mood had him searching for a tactful way to get them away from the dunes and to a more suitable place for a night of lovemaking.

Her eyes were half-closed, her expression one of sensual pleasure. Near the explosive stage himself, he couldn't stop himself from going further, sand or no sand. Bunching her blouse above her breasts, he dipped his head to lick and suck her nipples. "You are so beautiful. So beautiful," he whispered. But the sand on his tongue couldn't be ignored. "Cassie, honey, we have to go somewhere else."

Her voice was as weak as her limbs, though rife with erotic undertones. "Go where?"

He tried to make light of it and gave a small, dry laugh. "Away from this sand. Unless you have a blanket in your car."

Memory hit Cass hard and swiftly. There'd been a blanket in the Jeep that long-ago night, still there from a picnic a few days prior. Tonight there was no blanket, and she was suddenly aware of the sand in her hair, on her bare arms and legs, seeping under her clothes.

There was a major decision to be faced, and now, Cass realized. Gard was all but lying on top of her. The masculine contours of his body were not only apparent, they were chafing every erogenous zone she possessed. Her own feverish blood demanded a simple "Yes, we'll go somewhere else."

And yet... and yet...

"Let's get out of this sand," she said, shaken to her soul.

Was that a yes or a no? Frowning, Gard peered into her eyes. There was so much he couldn't say to her, sore subjects that would demolish her passion as quickly as one snuffed a match. And he wanted her passion more than he'd ever wanted anything. There was more. He admired her artistic talent, her pretty face and incredible body, the intelligence in her beautiful green eyes.

But it was her passion he ached for now, her lips under his, her nipples hard and sensitive because he had touched them, the heat and moisture that he knew lay between her thighs.

"Let me up, Gard," Cass whispered.

He had no choice now but to do as she asked. The decision was hers. Either she would go somewhere else with him or she wouldn't. He moved to the sand, telling himself encouragingly that she didn't seem angry, and that she was every bit as aroused as he was.

Getting to his feet, he helped Cass to hers. They brushed away sand from their clothes. Cass turned her head to the side and ruffled it with her fingers to get rid of the sand. Neither said anything. Gard was afraid of saying the wrong thing and Cass was fighting a ponderous inner battle.

Together they trudged through the sand to the parking area. Cass leaned against the trunk of her car to remove her shoes and shake out the sand, feverishly aware of Gard watching her every movement.

He came closer. "Cassie..."

"Give... me a minute," she said unsteadily. "I need to think." She stepped back into her shoes.

Gard acted on instinct. A minute for Cass to think could undermine every gain they had made tonight. He closed the gap between them with one big step and pulled her into his arms.

Instantly her heart went crazy again. "Gard..."

Tipping back her head, he pressed his lips to hers. His fingertips caressed her cheek, but when her mouth opened for his tongue, his hand slid downward, and this time it didn't stop moving until it was under her skirt and between her legs.

She gasped, but his hot kisses had her mindless and functioning on a primal level. He pressed into her, urging her backward. It took a moment to catch on, but by then she was lying against the sloped trunk of her own car and his hand was inside her panties. Part of her went into shock; the other part was bubbling like molten lava in a volcanic crater.

Her mouth opened to speak, though she wasn't sure what she had intended to say. It didn't matter, because Gard's mouth was hot and heavy on hers and causing the most delicious spirals of pleasure throughout her body.

Or was it his hand doing that? She could feel how wet she was because his fingers were wet. Her panties were obviously gone, but when? And how? Dazed and dizzy, she clutched at him, her own hands shaking, while little cries began and ended in her throat. She heard the rasp of his zipper and then his voice, deep and gravelly. "Bear with me a second, honey." The next sound was a snap of rubber, and the next sensation was of his hard body sliding into hers.

"Oh, Gard," she moaned. "We shouldn't be doing this."

Gard stopped. "Do you mean that?"

"Yes...no." Her head rolled back and forth on the cool, metal trunk. "I don't know." If he stopped now... He *couldn't* stop now. Not now. Not when she was on fire and nearly delirious with need of him. "No...I don't mean it," she whispered raggedly.

He curled into her. "Put your legs around me, sweetheart."

She obeyed and felt him pull her hips forward. His breathing was loud in her ear, but then he kissed her and began moving slowly inside her, and she no longer heard his gasping breaths or her own.

"It's good, so good," Gard whispered. "Is it good for you?"

"Yes . . . yes."

"I'm not hurting you, am I?"

"No . . . no. Nothing hurts, nothing." Clenching her legs tightly around him, she felt bonded to him in the closest possible fit. "Oh, Gard . . . Gard."

"I'm with you, honey."

She had yanked the tails of his shirt out of his sagging jeans. Almost greedily her hands roamed the taut skin of his back. Her eyes opened to look up at the moon and the stars, but all of life's true pleasures were within herself at the moment and her lids dropped again.

Way back in the most secret chambers of her mind was the knowledge that she was going to regret this, probably even more than she had the first time she had succumbed to Gard's seemingly invincible charm. Obviously she was a fool where Rebel Sterling was concerned.

She sighed, then moaned, because the universe was suddenly splintering into a million beautiful pieces. "Oh . . . oh . . . *oh!*"

Gard felt the same earthquake, the same tremors. "Oh, Cassie!"

A delicious weakness spread throughout her body. Her whole car had been rocking and rolling, and now it was as still as a statue. Still and silent.

Gard wished he never had to move again, partly from being so drained he could hardly wiggle a finger, but mostly because he had an unpleasant feeling in his gut that Cassandra was not going to come out of this all sweetness and light.

Gingerly he raised his head and smiled. "Hi." That seemed safe enough.

Cass was staring at his face, which was just barely visible in the distant pinpoints of light provided by Mother Nature. Indistinct as it was, that face was the most gorgeous she had ever seen. Maybe Gard was too handsome, she told herself in an attempt to find something wrong with his looks. He couldn't be as perfect as he put on these days, gorgeous and a solid citizen, to boot. She had to find something about him to fault. Either that or shoulder the blame for this fiasco herself.

"Everything okay?" Gard asked in as casual a voice as he could manage. If by some miracle she said something loving right now, no telling where they might end up. His feelings for her were getting serious, he knew, and if she was thinking the same about him...

"You weigh a ton," she said frostily. "And my back is killing me. Let me up."

Gard's hopes withered. "Sure, baby, anything you say."

The tone of his voice, hinting at male condescension and smugness, was all the spark needed to ignite the tinder of Cass's anger. Granted, it was mostly self-directed, but she didn't feel so kindly toward Gard right at the moment to mention that fact.

"You snake," she said, low and tensely.

Gard broke all contact with her, turned his back and walked away. Cass struggled to get herself upright. Her back *was* hurting. Who ever heard of making love on the trunk of a car, for God's sake? Of course, it wasn't Gard's body that had been bent backward for Lord knew how long. He *was* a snake, completely indifferent to her discomfort as long as he got what *he* wanted.

Sliding down till her feet were on the ground, Cass straightened her clothing while peering into the dark to see where Gard had gone, without success. Then she began looking for her panties and finally found them hanging on a low bush. Shoving them into the pocket of her skirt, she darted around to the driver's door of her car with every intention of driving away before Gard showed up again and demanded conversation. Her behavior tonight had been vulgar and demeaning, not because she had made love, but because she had made love with Gard Sterling. Again. In the same place as their first offense.

Her heart was pounding as she quietly opened the car door.

"Going somewhere?"

Cass whirled to see Gard descending upon her. "Stay away from me!"

He stopped and held up both hands. "I'm staying, I'm staying."

"And I'm leaving." Cass slid behind the wheel. She shot Gard a dirty look. "And don't pull any of your tricks, like getting in my car again. I'm going home, and nothing you can do or say is going to stop me."

"I wouldn't dream of even trying."

"Like hell you wouldn't." Cass fumbled with the key, paralleling her awkwardness at Gard's ranch. She began cussing under her breath because she seemed destined to make the same mistakes more than once with Gard.

Gard approached the open window. "Cassie, if you would turn on the overhead light, you might have better luck with the ignition."

Groaning, she laid her forehead on the steering wheel. "Why, dammit, why?"

Leaning over, Gard peered into the car. "What are you asking yourself, Cassandra, why you did it or why you liked it? The answer's probably the same to both questions."

Cass's head jerked up. "Don't you dare mention chemistry!"

"Well, what do you call it when a man and woman can't share a few simple kisses without going all the way?"

"We did *not* share a few simple kisses. You wouldn't recognize a simple kiss if one bit you on the nose." Disgusted with both him and herself, Cass waved him away. "Please . . . just leave me be. I want to sit here a minute before driving."

"Why are you angry, Cassie? Do you see what we did as sinful? Criminal? We're both unattached, aren't we?" When she didn't answer, he repeated with a little more force, "Aren't we? Cassandra, is there someone in Oregon?"

She almost lied and said yes, but instead she chose not to answer at all and started the engine with an unnecessary roar.

"Cassie, don't leave like this."

She sent him a brief but harsh look. "Do me a favor and make up your mind on that option so I never have to come back to Montana."

Watching her car speeding away, its tires kicking up dust, was like a knife in Gard's gut. Why had she made love with him if she hated him so much? What had he done fourteen years ago that she couldn't forgive or forget? It wasn't just the sex they had shared, it was something else. Something that had hurt her so badly, it was like a fresh wound every time she thought of it.

It was probably a lot like he felt right now, stabbed and bleeding. How in hell did a guy atone for something that bad, when he couldn't remember what it was and the lady wouldn't talk about it?

Six

Using the phone in his den, a room that did double duty as the ranch's office, Gard called the Whitfield ranch around nine the following morning. He was told by Julia Hayes, the Whitfield housekeeper whom he'd known for many years, "Cass left for Oregon, Gard."

"Already?" His stomach sank clear to his toes.

"She had a very early flight and left the house before daylight."

She had moved awfully damned fast, Gard thought with intense disappointment, apparently taking the first flight out. For some reason, although she had said she was going home, he hadn't visualized it happening so quickly.

"Thanks, Julia. Talk to you later." He put down the phone and sat back in his chair, discomfited by the mish-mash of emotions darting through his system. Cass was gone. Did that mean he wouldn't see her for the three months she had said he could take to make that decision? Maybe it meant more than that. Maybe she intended *never* to return to Montana. It was entirely possible, after all, to handle the sale of the Whitfield ranch—whether he or someone else bought it—through real estate agents, attorneys and the U.S. mail.

That idea wasn't only disturbing, it was totally unacceptable. In fact, it made Gard grit his teeth. In a surprisingly short period of time Cassandra had become important, and he couldn't live out the rest of his life with only a fleeting if earthshaking memory for company.

Scowling, he got up from his desk to pace the den. What could he do to bring her back to Montana? Going to Oregon and knocking on her door held a certain amount of appeal, but if she decided to slam it in his face he would have made the long trip for nothing. No, the key to any kind of future for the two of them lay in getting her back here. There had to be a way.

After nearly a half hour of pondering and discarding various ideas, he returned to his desk and dialed his lawyer's number, which was answered by a receptionist. It took a few minutes for George Mathews to come on the line. "Sorry to keep you waiting, Gard. I was on another call."

"No problem, George. I need your opinion on something." Gard detailed Cass's decision to give him another three months on that option. "Can she do that? Set a time limit at her discretion, I mean?"

"The contract recites only 'reasonable time,' Gard, so, no, she can't set a time limit to please herself. She's probably trying to pull a bluff. Or maybe her attorney told her to set a deadline and if you didn't respond within it, then they would force the issue in court."

"She said something like that," Gard confirmed. "George, I'm not going to make that decision in three months."

"So you *want* it to come to a court battle?"

"No, that's not what I want at all." He wasn't going to explain that what he did want was Cassandra Whitfield back in Montana, because that was personal and between Cass and him. "I really don't think it will come to that, but if it does, I'll deal with it then. Right now I'd like you to write a letter to Cassandra. She returned to Oregon, so send it to her home there. I want you to tell her very clearly that I do not agree to the three months, and that I'm thinking along the lines of two to three years."

"A letter like that will cause fireworks, Gard."

Gard smiled. "Probably will."

"Well, if that's what you want, I'll get the letter out today. It should go to her lawyer, though."

"Is it illegal to send it directly to her?"

"Not illegal, just a bit unethical."

"Do you object to writing her directly?"

There was a moment of silence, then George said, "If you don't mind a copy being mailed to her lawyer, no, I don't object."

"Sounds okay to me. I appreciate your help, George. Thanks. Oh, by the way, send me a copy, too."

Still smiling, Gard hung up. If that didn't get Cassandra's attention, nothing would.

For two days, ever since Cass got home, the sector of the Oregon coast in which her house was located had been foggy and cold. On the third morning she stood at the wide bank of windows of her third-floor studio with a cup of hot cocoa and frowned at the thick fog outside. She could see nothing *but* the soupy gray fog, which was so dense she could have been transplanted to another planet and not have known it. Even the sound of the ocean was muffled to the point of ear strain, and as for light in the studio, the ceiling lights were doing little more than casting ghostly shadows. It was impossible to work under these conditions, and she felt frustrated and impatient with the situation.

Glancing up at the ceiling she wondered about higher voltage bulbs. But in this old place, which despite her renovations was *still* an old place, high-voltage light fixtures would undoubtedly entail additional power being brought into the house. It wasn't the cost of such an endeavor that bothered Cass, but she wasn't in the mood for workmen and tools everywhere she looked.

In fact, she thought with a heavy sigh, she really wasn't in the mood for much of anything. Even if the sun had been glaringly bright and the studio lit up like a Christmas tree, would she be able to produce any work worth keeping? After all, she had worked during foggy spells before.

Walking over to the easel upon which resided the painting she had been attempting to finish since her return, she studied the work with a critical eye. It was mediocre at best, not even close to her usual standard of artistic professionalism. It was... She searched for the word and came up with *dull.* Dull and boring. Blaming the fog and bad lighting was a cop-out. Art came from within the person wielding the brush, and apparently there was nothing inside of her at the present to *put* on canvas.

The thought made her angry and determined to paint as she normally did. Setting down her cup of cocoa, she took the partially filled canvas from the easel and replaced it with a fresh one. Her oils were spread out on a high table at her right, along with dozens of brushes, paint thinner, several palettes and palette knives—most of the tools of her trade. All she had to do was get started. She stared at the blank canvas, then closed her eyes in an attempt to visualize a scene, any scene, or a mood, a feeling, something that would get her creative juices flowing.

Her eyes opened with a spark of anger. The only feeling she could readily grasp was the one she had brought home with her, utter disgust. How could she have been such a fool again with Gard? Lord Almighty, had she lost her mind the other night at the dunes? She had never been promiscuous nor—she'd always believed—stupid, so what had come over her to behave like a complete moron? If she never saw Gard Sterling again it would be too soon.

And yet... No! she thought with an almost violent toss of her head. She was not going to romanticize a sexual escapade that never should have happened. Hadn't she learned anything from her first go-around with Gard? How many men could make love at night and forget it before morning?

Well, this time she was going to be the one doing the forgetting, and to hell with what Gard might think of her attitude.

Glaring at the blank canvas, Cass gave up on getting any work done this morning and went down the two flights of stairs to the first floor. There were always household chores awaiting attention, because when she *was* in the mood for painting, it came first. Eyeing the layer of dust that had gathered on every piece of furniture during her long absence, she got out the vacuum cleaner and a stack of dust cloths.

But then she stopped herself from diving into the cleaning and sighed. She had been putting off that call to Francis, and it wasn't at all fair of her when she had promised to keep Francis informed. Going to her desk in the first-floor study, she dialed the Deering Gallery's number.

Francis, herself, answered. "Good morning. Deering Gallery."

"Hi, Francis. It's me, Cass. Have you got a minute to talk?"

"Sure, go ahead."

"Well . . . it's not good news, Francis. Sterling isn't budging and my lawyer advised me to give him another three months. I don't expect you to wait that long, so I guess I'm really calling to apologize for holding you up as long as I did."

"Oh . . . well . . ."

Cass frowned. Francis Deering was not a woman who stammered over anything. Cass had honestly anticipated a bluntly stated "I guess that's that, then, Cass." Instead she was hearing reluctance and a bit of confusion in Francis's voice.

"Listen, Cass," Francis said. "I gave you first shot at that fifty percent and I'm willing to keep the offer open. Who knows? Sterling might change his mind tomorrow."

Cass was truly stunned. "Well, this is great, Francis. I never would have asked. I mean, you've always been so adamant about wanting the transaction completed right away."

"I know. But I really would like you to be my partner. The others...well, to heck with them. Actually, what I'll do is tell them I've given you more time. Simple."

"I can't thank you enough," Cass said slowly, not quite able to grasp Francis's change of attitude.

"So," Francis said, "will you be staying in Montana for the three months?"

"I'm back home, Francis."

"Oh, you are. Well, in that case I'll be watching for the snapshots of some new Whitfield canvases."

Snapshots was how Cass let Francis know she had completed a painting. Cass smiled weakly. "Don't watch too closely, Francis. I've been having a little trouble getting started."

"Understandable, considering the past few months, Cass."

They chatted a few more minutes before hanging up, then Cass sat there thinking about Francis's turnabout. Until this conversation, Francis had been totally inflexible regarding the sale of that fifty percent. Odd, Cass thought.

But it was definitely in her favor, odd or not. Getting up, she headed for the vacuum cleaner and dust cloths.

An hour later Cass's doorbell rang. Surprised because she hadn't called any of her local friends to let them know she was home, she hurried to see who was on her front porch. It was, of all people, the mailman.

Cass hurriedly opened the door. "Hi, Joe."

"Hello, Cass. Got a special delivery for you. You gotta sign for it." Joe held out a pen and the package. "Sign on the line with the *X*."

"Right." Cass scrawled her signature and Joe tore off the receipt and passed her the package. "Thanks, Joe."

"You're welcome. Nasty weather, huh?" He started from the porch.

"Sure is. I'm getting very tired of fog."

"Same here. See ya."

Cass closed the door and examined the package, which from its shape and size could only contain a letter. Then she saw the sender's information and her eyes narrowed. A special-delivery letter from Gard's attorney? What was going on here?

Hastily she tore open the package and pulled out an envelope, which bore the embossed name and address of George Mathews, Attorney At Law. From it, she extracted one neatly folded sheet of paper. It was a letter.

Dear Miss Whitfield,

At the request of my client, Mr. Gardiner Sterling, I am writing to inform you of his response to your three-month time limit with regard to the buy/sell option in the contract between Ridge Whitfield and Loyal Sterling.

Mr. Gardiner Sterling declines your time limit, and has stated that he requires at least two years to exercise that option, and possibly three. In as much as the contract's only reference to time recites "reasonable time," Mr. Sterling feels well within his rights to take whatever time is necessary for him to make a sound and sensible decision.

A copy of this letter is being mailed to your attorney, Mr. Peter Addington, and to Mr. Sterling.

Sincerely,
George Mathews

With her blood pressure rising, Cass read the letter a second time. Two to three years? Did Gard actually think she would stand by and do nothing while he procrastinated ad infinitum? And just when she had renewed hopes for buying into the Deering Gallery again. How dare he do this! Thinking of a whole slew of impolite names to call him, she marched to the phone and dialed the long-distance number of her own lawyer. Naturally she had been forced to hire a Montana attorney, which was one of the reasons she had stayed in Montana for so long after her father's death, to be in close contact with Peter Addington.

To her annoyance, Peter was out of his office, but his secretary assured her that he would return her call as soon he returned.

Waiting for that call drove Cass up the wall. Her anger mounted with each passing minute. Two to three years, indeed! She wasn't going to put up with it, and that was final.

An hour later her telephone finally rang. "Cassandra? Peter Addington. Kelly said you called."

"I most certainly did call. Peter, did you receive a copy of the letter George Mathews sent me? By special delivery, no less," she fumed.

"Not yet I haven't. But I haven't gone through my mail yet today. Let me check, Cass. Hold on." Cass could hear him calling, "Kelly? Is there a letter from George Mathews in today's mail?"

There was some muffled conversation on Peter's end, indicating to Cass that he had laid down the phone. Then he came back on the line. "Yes, I have it. Give me a minute to read it." A moment of silence ensued. "Well, now," Peter said. "How do you feel about this?"

"How do I feel? I'm so angry I could spit, that's how I feel. Gard can't do this, can he?"

"Apparently he thinks he can. I suppose it's no worse than your setting that three-month deadline, Cass. The bottom line, of course, is that if the two of you can't come to an amicable agreement on an interpretation of 'reasonable time,' you'll have to let a judge decide."

"Damn him!" Cass exploded. "He knows I want to sell right away, not three years from now. He's doing this just to get my goat."

"Why would he do that?"

"Uh, to cause trouble. He's arrogant and always has been. He would probably drag this out even if he *knew* he was going to end up buying the place, just to annoy me."

"Well, apparently he's succeeded in that effort," Peter said dryly. "Cass, is this thing turning into some kind of personal problem between you and Gardiner Sterling?"

Cass drew an exasperated breath. "I suppose you could say that."

"That's unfortunate, because there are perfectly legal ways to delay a court decision for years. This might best be resolved by direct contact between yourself and Mr. Sterling. Unless, of course, you prefer going through the legal system. I'm prepared to petition the court for a decision whenever you say, but considering what you've told me, *you* must be prepared for a long, drawn-out contest."

"Oh, great," Cass muttered. She didn't want any more direct contact with Gard, damn his black soul, of which he was fully cognizant. But that was probably the very reason he was doing this, to *force* her to contact him again.

She suddenly didn't want to talk to Peter Addington, Attorney At Law, any longer. "I'll call again, Peter. Thanks for your time." Hanging up, she thought wryly that Peter Addington would receive all the thanks he deserved when he billed her. To put it bluntly, he hadn't accomplished one damned thing in her behalf. For that matter, Gard's attorney had accomplished about the same for him. What she probably should have done the minute she learned of that contract was to go to Gard and attempt to settle the issue without involving lawyers.

But she hadn't wanted to face Gard for any reason. Cass sighed despondently. She still didn't, but neither did she want this ridiculous situation to dominate the next three years of her life.

Switching on the vacuum cleaner, she viciously thrust the machine under tables and around the sofa and chairs in her living room. Knowing how neatly Gard had put her on the spot was infuriating, an emotion that resulted in a spanking-clean carpet in her living room, plus a throbbing headache.

By that evening Cass had thought the situation through from every conceivable angle. Her conclusions weren't particularly comforting, but then, neither was the situation. Gard was obviously going to be a horse's behind about the contract, and she could stoop to his level and give him one hell of a fight in court, she could simply ignore him until he made up his mind, however long he took, or she could do what Peter had suggested: attempt to reach an amicable interpretation of the term "reasonable time" with Gard, *out* of court.

Of course, her third option couldn't be accomplished with her in Oregon and Gard in Montana, which meant returning to the Whitfield ranch, *which* Cass resented to the point of calling Gard a few more impolite names under her breath every time she thought of it. Actually the names she mumbled were plain vile, and she didn't feel any guilt over it, either. She could very easily strangle Mr. Rebel Sterling if he were within reach, which was another reason the idea of returning to his territory was so disturbing. Keeping her temper under control if and when she met with him again just might prove to be impossible, and the picture in her mind of her screeching like a banshee at him was extremely unsettling.

However, ignoring his ludicrous demands and letting him take years to make that decision rubbed her so wrong, she *already* felt like screeching. She was so upset that when her usual bedtime approached, she knew she would never go to sleep, so she climbed the stairs to her studio. The ceiling lights seemed to throw more light at night, and many times she had painted after dark.

Tonight she just didn't give a damn if she produced something salable or not, and she squirted a big dollop of vermilion onto a palette, immediately followed by several others: royal blue, deep purple, kelly green, stark white and black. Fuming, she began to slash the blank canvas with a thick brush loaded with vermilion. Rinsing the brush, she dried it and reloaded with the purple. Never had she ever worked without first thinning the paint and mixing colors to attain delicate hues and textures. What she was doing was simply letting off steam, and about an hour passed before she frowned at the canvas, stepped back and took a really good look. The colors seemed to leap off the canvas, as well as the design.

Cass's mouth literally dropped open for a moment before she whispered, "Abstract expressionism." Certainly the bold colors and radical design expressed the emotions she had been feeling while wielding the brush. But she had never tried this style of painting before, and what she had created was actually startling.

It was also very exciting. Picking up a much smaller brush, she streaked a little white here and there, just minute touches to highlight the overall design. Her gaze roamed the painting and it was stunning to realize that she liked it.

But...would anyone else? Francis, in particular? Francis was always blunt with her opinions. If something was good, she said so in glowing terms. If not, her bluntness gave the artist no option but to trust her judgment.

Their arrangement was quite simple. Whenever Cass produced a painting she felt had merit, she took a picture of it to send to Francis. Oil paints dried slowly and canvases had to be carefully crated for shipment. Francis could tell from a snapshot whether or not she wanted to view the actual painting.

Worrying her thumbnail with her teeth, Cass studied the painting and tried to see it through Francis's eyes. It was impossible to do, of course, and she decided to wait until morning before making a decision about sending a snapshot to San Francisco.

Quickly then, she began cleaning her brushes and palette. She was almost through when she stopped dead in her tracks with a startling thought. Whether or not the painting was an artistic success, doing it had soothed her ruffled emotions. She actually felt calm and collected, whole again. How strange. Not that she hadn't felt satisfaction from other paintings—intense satisfaction from some—but never had she felt as she did now.

"Hmm," she said, thinking about it while finishing the cleaning of her very expensive brushes.

After another long look at the painting, she turned out the lights and descended to the second floor and her bedroom. Yawning, she was certain that she could sleep now.

But once in bed and physically very comfortable, her thoughts returned to Gard and the dirty trick he had pulled on her. Two to three years to make that decision was preposterous, which he had to know as well as she did. Was he *trying* to draw her into a legal battle? What possible gain would he receive from out-and-out warfare?

"Humph," she muttered. Trying to figure out what went on in that man's overly macho, swelled head was a waste of time. At least she knew one thing now: she didn't want a long, drawn-out legal hassle with attorneys and judges and court appearances.

But neither could she ignore Gard's abominable attitude for two to three years. Gard probably thought she had inherited a fortune in cash from her father, but that wasn't even remotely true. Yes, there had been some cash in the estate, but not anything like she had expected. Ridge Whitfield had made a lot of money over the years, but apparently he had also spent a lot of money. More than likely Gard didn't realize that, because she certainly hadn't.

Sighing, Cass turned over in bed and stared at the dark ceiling. There was really only one sensible course for her to take, and that was to return to Montana to try to make Gard understand how badly she needed to sell, possibly even tell him about her plans to buy into the Deering Gallery.

At that thought a shiver went up Cass's spine, and it wasn't altogether from dread over facing Gard again.

But she certainly wasn't thinking of anything personal between tween them, was she? Another go-around such as had occurred at the dunes? Gard was a dangerous man where she was concerned, which he'd proven twice in her lifetime. Did she want *more* proof?

When that letter arrived today she could have gleefully murdered Gard Sterling, and now she was remembering how his body had felt on hers, in hers, while she was sprawled on the trunk of a car.

Hell, she *was* demented, no question about it.

Seven

Gard was on the phone with his lawyer. "George, it's been almost two weeks since Cassandra Whitfield got your letter and she hasn't responded. At least, I haven't heard anything from her. Have you?"

"No, I haven't, Gard."

"Well, what do you think about her silence?"

"Apparently she's accepting your ultimatum."

Gard frowned. "I really can't believe she would do that. Listen, George, I want you to contact her again. Tell her that I'm insisting on her agreement to my terms in writing."

"In writing? Gard, my advice is to leave her be. If she's going along with your two- to three-year time limit on that contract, a demand of that sort could very likely stir up a hornet's nest of trouble."

"Nothing we can't handle, I'm sure. Please write the letter, George."

After hanging up, Gard had to chuckle. He was confusing poor old George, but that was the way the ball was bouncing and couldn't be helped.

Every day Cass had been attempting another such dramatic, passionate painting as she had produced the night she'd been so angry, and every day she failed. Oh, she created some pretty designs and colorful canvases, but none of them had the passion, energy and emotion of the first one. It was terribly frustrating, making her doubt her talent, making her think the original abstract was a fluke and possibly her one and only success as far as abstract expressionism went.

She would stare at that painting with her heart in her throat and a feeling of awe. Although she had taken the snapshots and they were ready for mailing, she couldn't bring herself to send them to Francis. For one thing, she wasn't sure she wanted to sell her abstract. Quite literally, she had fallen in love with it, something that had never occurred with any of her other paintings.

Second, should Francis like it and want more of the same, Cass had nothing else to show her. The result of this quandary was that she was producing nothing. Her old style of work, softly muted colors and fine, wispy textures, seemed bland and uninteresting now. She spent many hours walking the rocky beach, pondering the situation, and worrying about it. If an artist didn't produce art, was she still an artist?

She had finally gotten around to calling a few friends, but get-togethers had lost their flavor—probably because her mind was elsewhere—and she found that she preferred being alone. Somehow she had to get back on track with her work, whichever direction it took.

On a Wednesday she was surprised by another special-delivery packet, again from George Mathews.

Frowning, she tore it open and extracted the letter.

Dear Miss Whitfield,

My client, Gardiner Sterling, requires your agreement in writing to his two- to three-year time limit on the buy/sell option in the contract between your father and his. I have drawn up a simple document stating your approval, which is enclosed. Your signature, where designated, will satisfy Mr. Sterling and legalize the agreement. A pre-addressed, stamped envelope is enclosed for your convenience.

Sincerely,
George Mathews

Instant fury struck Cass. Gard just couldn't let well enough alone, could he? He was going to push and push until she fought back, and in her present state of mind, worrying about her work and all, she was just about there. Well, Gard could shove this "simple document" up his nose. Hell would freeze over before she'd sign it, and maybe she would like to tell him so in person.

Yes, why not? Cass thought angrily. She sure wasn't getting anything done here.

By that evening she had her travel arrangements made and her suitcases packed. There was one that hadn't accompanied her on any of her previous trips to the ranch, a large case containing paint and blank canvases. Hopefully she could get some work done in Montana, in between fighting with Gard, of course. *That* unpleasant prospect had top priority.

Cass deplaned in Billings and immediately looked for Jake Little, the ranch foreman. She had called the ranch yesterday and told Julia, the housekeeper, to have Jake meet her plane. Julia had agreed, then mentioned, "If Jake can't do it for some reason, I'll be there, Cass."

But neither Jake nor Julia was at the gate. "Hmm," she murmured, wondering if there had been a misunderstanding on the time of her arrival.

Then she froze. Coming toward her was Gard, wearing a somber expression that evolved into a tentative smile as he got closer. He stopped in front of her. "Hi."

Cass was dumbfounded. "What are you doing here?"

"Picking you up."

"Picking me up! What happened to Jake? Or Julia? Why would *you* be picking me up?"

Gard shifted his weight, standing in a casual pose. "I just happened to drop by your ranch yesterday afternoon to ask Julia if she'd heard from you, and..."

Cass was livid. "You pumped *my* housekeeper for information about me?"

"No pumping, Cass. Just normal conversation. Julia's an old friend."

"You rat," Cass said in an undertone. If they weren't in a public place, she wouldn't be speaking so quietly, rest assured. "You've got more gall than anyone I've ever known."

"Possibly," Gard said as calmly as could be. "Julia said you were flying in today, and since I was coming to Billings anyway, I told her I would be happy to save her and Jake the trip."

"How sweet," Cass said sarcastically. "How benevolent."

"You're angry."

"How can you tell?" Cass looked away, fuming internally, and wondered about renting a car and letting this overbearing snake in the grass drive back to the valley by himself.

"I hope you're not angry with Julia," Gard said.

"Julia?" Cass's eyes flashed around to his. "Julia has nothing to do with this. I can just see you pulling information out of her and then making your generous, neighborly offer to help her out. No, Gard, I'm not angry with Julia."

"Then it must be me."

"Oh, stop acting like you just figured out the answer to some idiotic puzzle," Cass snapped. "I'm going to get my luggage. You do whatever suits your fancy." She took off walking.

Grinning slightly, Gard followed. He'd suspected she would be ticked off about this, hoping otherwise, of course. But Cass's anger was almost tangible, and it wasn't all because of his being at the gate instead of Julia or Jake. She had arrived angry and he couldn't blame her.

But at least she was here. His written demands had worked exactly as he had hoped they would. She was back in Montana, where he wanted her, and eventually he would get everything straightened out between them.

At the luggage carousel Cass stood with a cold, forbidding expression, waiting for her suitcases to appear. Renting a car to drive herself to the ranch would mean that someone would have to bring it back to Billings, an irritating fact that she knew was going to force her into Gard's truck for the trip to the valley. The thought of seventy miles of confinement with him grated on her nerves. Of course, setting him straight was why she was here at all, so maybe this was as good a time as any to do it.

Gard had been standing two steps behind Cass, admiring her taupe slack suit and pretty hair. When the carousel started up and the luggage began tumbling off of the conveyor, he moved to stand beside her. "Point out yours and I'll get it for you."

She sent him a dirty look. "Don't be polite to me, Gard. We both know you don't mean it."

He cocked an eyebrow. "Oh? So now you're a mind reader?"

"I don't have to be a mind reader to know when I'm being railroaded." Spotting one of her suitcases, Cass moved to the carousel and reached for it. Gard literally wrested it from her hand, and her only thanks was a venomous look. They went through the same inane routine with the rest of her things, and it was then that Cass told herself to calm down. Whether or not she was justifiably angry with Gard, they were, after all, in a public place. Second, she was certainly mature enough to deal with the situation without throwing tantrums.

She began her cold war by stepping back and giving him the freedom to pick up the largest pieces of her luggage. "I'll carry those," she said, indicating the two smallest cases.

Gard nodded. "Right." It thrilled him that she hadn't arrived with only one small overnight case. Obviously she had packed for an extended visit.

They were in his truck and leaving Billings when Cass pulled a piece of paper from her purse. "You really don't expect me to sign this ludicrous document, do you?" Through supreme effort, she sounded almost normal.

He took his eyes from the road and briefly glanced at the paper. "The only documented agreement is between our fathers. There should be something in writing between us, Cass."

"Our only agreement seems to be to disagree," she answered. "Which, I might add, is all your doing." Regardless of the conversation being focused on that old contract, Cass was all too aware of Gard as a man. It was much easier to hate him when she wasn't sitting within two feet of him, she realized uneasily. And the fact that they had made love, not once but twice, and that the second time was still very fresh in her memory, wasn't aiding her composure.

"All my doing, huh?" Gard mused out loud. "Do you think I'm handling our situation badly?"

"Well, you're certainly not making it easy for me," Cass retorted.

"That does bother me, you know. You're the last person I'd ever want to hurt. But business is business, Cass."

She sighed, remembering Francis saying those exact words. But then, she also remembered Francis's startling reversal. Why would the gallery owner initially demand a quick sale and then back down? If Ridge Whitfield were still alive, what would he say about Francis's change in attitude? Certainly it was something Cass would have discussed with her father. She never had claimed to understand business, having dedicated her life to art. Buying into the gallery had merely seemed like an extension of her chosen profession, and now she wasn't so sure of that.

But there was little point to worrying about that aspect of her life until she settled this thing with Gard, Cass thought resentfully. If it didn't get settled, she would never own anything but the Whitfield ranch.

"Your coming back really surprised me," Gard commented, lying through his teeth.

Cass sent him a look. "I don't believe you. I think you engineered the whole thing. Let's get one thing straight right now, Gard. You might have forced me back here with your ridiculous demands, but there isn't going to be any foolishness between us."

"Foolishness? You mean like what happened at the dunes?"

Cass's face colored. "You know exactly what I mean."

"Hmm. Well, it's funny how two people interpret the same incident, isn't it? You consider what we did as foolish, and I—"

"Just drop it! I'm not the least bit interested in your interpretation of what happened. Just remember that it's not going to be repeated. I'm back in Montana for only one reason, and that's to get that contract resolved. I will not sign this—" Cass waved the piece of paper from George Mathews "—agreement under any circumstances, which leaves us exactly where we were when I flew home a few weeks ago.

"Let me say something else. I'm reneging on the three months I gave you before to make up your mind. I want an answer now, and I swear on my father's memory that if you don't give me one, I'll have my lawyer file a lawsuit against you for every asset you own. You cannot bring my life to a standstill just because you're too damned wishy-washy to make a decision. What's more—"

Gard cut in. "Hey, slow down. If you'd let me get a word in edgewise—"

"So you can come up with more excuses for delay? You're not going to talk me into any more delays, so don't waste your breath."

"In other words, I either give you an answer right now or you're calling your attorney when you get to the ranch."

"Not other words, Gard, *same* words."

"Tell you what," he said, turning the pickup into the parking area of a roadside gas station. "There's a pay phone." He braked to a stop and turned in the seat to face Cass. "Why put it off one minute longer than you have to? Make your call."

Cass was thunderstruck and silent, but only for a moment. Her eyes narrowed furiously. "You have no intention of cooperating, do you? If you had the slightest idea of how much I despise you right now..."

"Why? Because I called your bluff?"

That was it, of course, although Cass would die before admitting it. But another use for that phone suddenly came to mind, and she reached for the door handle. Her getting out and marching to the phone booth gave Gard a start. He, too, had been bluffing, and had never dreamed that she would actually call her attorney from here.

Cass dropped some coins into the phone and dialed a number. "Whitfield ranch," said a woman.

"Julia? This is Cass. I'm about halfway to the ranch, at Logan's Service Station. Would you come and get me?" Gard might consider Julia an old friend, but so did she, Cass thought snidely. She and Julia had become especially close during her long stay at the ranch after her father died, so she felt no qualms about requesting Julia to make the drive.

"You're stuck out there? What happened? Did Gard's truck break down?"

"None of the above," Cass replied. "I'll explain when I see you. Can you come right away?"

"Well, of course. I'll get my purse and leave immediately."

"Thanks, Julia."

Cass hung up and walked out of the booth with a completely blank expression. Gard was watching her closely, thinking that had been an awfully short conversation to initiate a lawsuit.

Then she surprised him again by going to the back of the pickup instead of getting in. He hopped out and hurried to the rear of his rig. Cass was opening the tailgate. "What in hell are you doing?"

"Removing my luggage."

"Why?"

"Because I refuse to ride one more mile with you, that's why," she said shortly. "Julia's picking me up."

"Cass, this is silly. Call Julia back. I'll take you home."

"Never," Cass said coldly. She had succeeded in pulling her suitcases from the truck bed and setting them on the ground. Then she faced Gard with a menacing expression. "The only communication I want with you from here on in is through our lawyers. You're ruining my life and do you give a damn? Did it ever once occur to you that I might have a very good reason for wanting to sell the ranch? Even if I didn't, what gives you the right to manipulate the terms of that contract to suit yourself? You know as well as I do that neither of our fathers ever thought you and I would have this much trouble dealing with it. They were both honorable men, and 'reasonable time' to them didn't mean two to three years."

Gard took a long breath and looked off into the distance. Finally he brought his gaze back to her. "All right, you win. I'll give you an answer in two weeks. Guaranteed."

Her eyes narrowed suspiciously. "Guaranteed?"

"I just said so, didn't I? I have a condition, though."

"Now why aren't I surprised? What is it?"

"That you go camping with me."

Cass nearly choked. "That I what?"

"Go camping with me."

She shook her head in utter dismay. "You're crazy. In the first place, I hate camping. In the second, why would I go anywhere with you?"

"It's my condition, Cass. You'll have my answer in two weeks, if you spend it with me."

Her eyes widened. "You're talking about a *two-week* camping trip? My God, I would shrivel up and die in that length of time. I told you, I hate camping. Sleeping on the ground? Cooking on an open fire? The mere thought of living like that gives me cold chills." Despite her protestations, however, her mind was working. Couldn't she bear almost anything for two weeks to get this mess resolved?

But dare she trust his word? Her chin lifted. "Supposing...just supposing I agreed...would you put your guarantee in writing?"

"Sure would."

Frowning, Cass chewed on her bottom lip. "Uh, why?"

"Why, what?"

"Why do you want to take me camping? I told you there wasn't going to be anything personal between us ever again, so if that's what you're thinking..."

Gard shook his head. "No, that's not what I'm thinking. I'd just like us to spend some time together."

"But why camping?"

"Because we'd be off by ourselves. Best way I know of for two people to become friends."

"Friends?" Cass said incredulously. "That's what you want, for you and I to become friends?"

"That's it." Gard studied her doubting expression. "So, what do you say?"

She didn't know what to say. Frankly, she'd never been so completely addled in her life. "Um...give me a few minutes. I need to think." She walked away.

Gard sat on the tailgate of his pickup and watched her walking around, knowing fairly well what was going through her mind. Dare she trust him? Where would he take her for two weeks? What, really, was going on in his devious brain? He almost laughed, thinking of the many questions Cass must be wrestling with. He had been truthful with her to a point, and that point was when he'd declared that all he wanted was friendship from her.

Damn, she was pretty, marching around Logan's parking area like a little general. Pretty or not, why had he fallen so hard for her? It wasn't only the best sex of his life that had him plotting to get her attention. Not one of the other women who had passed through his life had affected him as Cass did. Maybe everyone had a secret place in their heart slated for one special person, but until Cass, he hadn't known about it. He knew about it now, and it was filled with thoughts of Cass, feelings for Cass, and memories that included their recent night at the dunes, though not exclusively. There was also the way she moved, the way she spoke—when she wasn't angry—the light in her beautiful green eyes, the curve of her lips. There was a warmth in his system he'd never felt before, simply because of Cass Whitfield.

Cass was struggling with Gard's proposition. It was ridiculous, of course, and only a self-centered, have-it-all-his-own-way man would ever come up with such a preposterous plan.

But what if it worked? What if he gave her an answer in two weeks? That was why she was here, wasn't it? The only reason? But two weeks in the woods. My God, could she bear it? And she had better not think that Gard wouldn't try something if they were off in the wilds together for that length of time. She would have to be on her guard every minute of those two weeks, an appalling idea.

Actually, she felt like an idiot for even considering giving in to Gard's blackmail. That was all it was, of course, and his reason for pulling this stunt—wanting them to be friends—was so inane that only a fool would believe it.

She stopped pacing to look over at him, where he was seated and waiting on the tailgate. He was looking at her, as well, and she had to ask herself what he really wanted from her. Asking him would be fruitless; he would rattle off another lie about friendship and she still wouldn't know.

But deep down, didn't she have a pretty good idea of what he would expect, or at least hope for, from an extended camp-out? Given the last time they had been alone together, that night at the dunes, could she doubt what was cooking in his scheming brain?

Frowning, she began walking again. Gard was watching every move she made, but her mind was so cluttered with indecision she was able to ignore his staring. Camping... Lord, she really did hate it. Her father had adored taking his sleeping bag, a few supplies and his fishing gear and heading for some out-of-the-way spot for a weekend. Her mother had rarely gone along, as she hadn't liked camping or fishing.

Then, when Cass was about sixteen, Ridge had insisted she go with him one weekend. She had put up an argument, but he'd been adamant. "You've got to try it at least once, Cassie. How will you know if you like camping if you don't try it? It might be right up your alley."

Reluctantly she had gone with him, and it definitely had *not* been "right up her alley." She had hated bathing in the woods, among even more personal necessities, hated sleeping on the ground, and loathed the bugs, the camp food and the isolation. It had been an awful two days, and she had vowed when it was over to never repeat the experience.

Thinking of two weeks of that kind of misery made Cass shudder. But hadn't she decided that she could stand anything for a few weeks to get this mess with Gard over and done with?

She still wasn't altogether sold, however, when she walked back to Gard and the pickup. "How about making it one week?"

Gard's pulse leapt. "Um...one week, huh?" He hadn't let himself believe that she would agree to spending *any* length of time with him, so this was a major victory in his book. He looked thoughtful for a moment, then said, "Tell you what. We'll set it for one week and if you like it, we can always extend it another week."

Cass's relief literally weakened her knees. She had just scored a major victory, since she knew there was no way she was going to "like it" and agree to a second week.

"And you'll put it in writing that I'll have your decision in two weeks, either way?"

"Two weeks from today. If we leave today, that is. If we go tomorrow, two weeks from then."

"Well, it makes better sense to go tomorrow," Cass said, thinking of her suitcases, which certainly would have to be repacked. After all, there was little point to taking lacy nightgowns, dresses and high-heeled pumps on a camping trip. She winced internally, envisioning the awful outing. Going tomorrow made *much* better sense. That way she would have tonight to think about Gard's game playing, and it wasn't out of the question for her to change her mind on the deal.

"Tomorrow it is." Gard slid from the tailgate to the ground. "Let's put your luggage back in the truck. We can watch for Julia's car on the way."

Cass checked her watch. "No, Julia should be along any minute. I'll wait for her. You don't have to wait, though."

"I'm not leaving you out here on the side of the road."

"Good heavens, I'm hardly in any danger." Cars had been pulling in and out of Logan's Service Station the whole time they'd been there. The truth was that she'd like to see Gard drive away and be alone for a while. He was manipulating her again, which definitely warranted some thought, and that could not be accomplished with his eyes boring holes into her.

"I'll wait," Gard stated in a voice that brooked no further argument. "How about a soda?"

Cass sighed. The man was like a barnacle. Once attached, there was no easy way to get rid of him. "Sure, why not? A diet cola, if they have it."

Gard left to enter Logan's building. Feeling down in the dumps, and as she'd told Gard, "railroaded," Cass leaned her hips against the tailgate and wished her father were alive. He had always been there to talk to, and she missed his earthy but sensible advice something terrible. To be honest, had she done anything right since his death? Maybe she should stop worrying about buying into the gallery. For some reason she had an uneasy feeling about that now.

But it was no worse than the uneasiness she felt over Gard's illogical demands. A camping trip, indeed. What would he come up with next?

Cass's spirits rose several notches when she saw Julia driving in. At the same time, Gard came walking out of the building with two cans of soda.

They all came together. Cass took the diet cola from Gard's hand with a terse, "Thanks," then set it down to go for her luggage. Julia's curious gaze went back and forth between Cass and Gard, but she merely unlocked the trunk of her car without asking any questions.

It was Gard who lifted the suitcases into the trunk after a brief, "Hi," to Julia. Cass hurriedly retrieved her soda and got into the passenger seat of the car. Julia walked around to the driver's side.

Gard held Cass's door so she couldn't close it. "What time in the morning?"

Cass took a breath. "You seem to be calling the shots, so what time do you suggest?"

"Around eight?"

She nodded. "All right."

Gard closed the door and backed away from the car. Julia got it turned around and heading toward the ranch. "Well, I certainly didn't expect to see Gard there," she said.

Cass sighed wearily. "It's a long, dull story, Julia, so I'll bring it down to its basics. Gard won't give me an answer on that buy/sell option unless I go camping with him for a week." She looked at the older woman. "What do you think of that?"

To her surprise, Julia was smiling. "Gard always did have a way about him, didn't he?"

"He sure did, as long as it was *his* way," Cass said with resentment in every syllable.

Eight

Cass was a tantalizing woman, Gard thought that night with his hands locked behind his head on the pillow and his eyes wide open and staring into the darkness of his bedroom. At least, she tantalized him. He kept thinking about her and came up with other complimentary adjectives: intriguing, beautiful, intelligent, sexy and artistic. She was a dynamite package, because he couldn't deny that she was also temperamental, argumentative and sometimes downright obnoxious. She would be a handful for any man, but why did he keep thinking that he brought out both the best and the worst in her? Maybe because she hadn't been able to say no that night at the dunes? From her mood afterward, it was damned obvious that she wished she *had* said no.

He was expecting something from the camping trip, but what, exactly? Was he in a marrying mood? Was that what was going on in the back of his mind? Had he finally found the one woman he didn't want to live without? The one with whom he wanted to share everything he was and was not? Was he ready for the big commitment and focusing that instinctual need on Cass?

That progression of thoughts led to one that he knew to be fact: the feelings he was undergoing were special and unique. If Cass hadn't come along again, he wouldn't be thinking about commitment, or sharing, or anything else, beyond completely casual sex, with any other woman, as he had done all of his adult life. No, this was different with Cass. He was different *because* of Cass.

Was he in love with her?

Frowning, Gard turned over in bed to face the open window and the moonlight beaming into the room. The question—was he in love?—once shaped and in the open, now seemed embedded in his brain. He suspected it was going to be a permanent part of himself from here on in, which, given the tone of Cass's and his present relationship, wasn't all that comforting.

All he could do was see what happened this week, right?

Right, he thought in an uneasy reply. Their week together would tell the tale.

The next morning Gard rapped on the Whitfield front door at eight sharp. Cass opened it and said a sober, terse, "Good morning," which didn't exactly elevate Gard's spirits.

But they had a week's adventure ahead of them, and Cass would come around. He was sure of it.

"Good morning," he said cheerfully. "Everything ready to go?"

Cass was tired from a sleepless night. At times during the dark hours she had become so furious over Gard's sneaky maneuvering that she swore to tell him to go to hell in the morning and then call Peter Addington with instructions to file the lawsuit.

But each time common sense prevailed. She winced at a mental picture of herself in court making accusations. *Gar-*

diner Sterling tried to blackmail me into spending a week in the woods with him. His attorney would object on some grounds, or hers would, or the judge would pound his gavel and tell all of them to shut up. The situation was too ludicrous to take public. Her best course—as infuriating as it was—was to go on that ridiculous camping trip and get it over with.

"Do you have the written guarantee you promised?" Cass asked coldly.

"Right here." Gard pulled a folded paper from his shirt pocket and handed it over.

Cass read it, decided the simple document would do, then noted that Gard's signature was witnessed by two people. "Who are these witnesses?"

"They work for me. Would you rather it be notarized? It would take us out of our way, but we could drive to town and have it notarized if you want."

"Wait here for a minute." Taking the document with her, Cass went to find Julia, whom she located in the kitchen. "Please look at this, Julia, and tell me if you recognize the names of the people who witnessed Gard's signature."

Julia took the paper and checked the names. She nodded. "Robert Sachs and James LeRoy. They've both worked on the Sterling ranch for years."

"Okay, thanks." Cass carried the paper to her bedroom, tucked it into a bureau drawer and returned to where Gard was waiting near the front door, studying her two pieces of luggage rather intently, which were also near the door. One was a normal suitcase and the other was a black canvas bag of peculiar dimensions. He had noticed it yesterday at the airport, of course, even handled it, but until now he hadn't questioned its contents. Whatever it contained, Cass obviously intended taking it with her.

"*Now* everything's ready to go," Cass stated, sweeping into the room.

"These are your bags, right?"

"Yes." Stifling his curiosity concerning the black bag, Gard picked up both.

Cass got the door, and out they went. It was a beautiful morning, for which she was grateful, with a clear sky and no threat of rain. Rainy weather would be a final straw to something she already abhorred, and suffering in pleasant weather wouldn't be quite as unbearable as suffering in the rain.

Outside she saw that the entire bed of Gard's pickup was neatly covered with a huge, clean tarp. By its bulges and bumps, it was obviously protecting his camping gear. She stood by and watched while he loosened one corner of the tarp and slid her luggage beneath it, then secured it again.

"All set," he announced, going around to the passenger door to open it for her.

"Thanks," she allowed without a bit of warmth, climbing in under her own steam.

"You're welcome." He closed the door and loped around the front of the truck to the driver's side.

They were well under way before either spoke. Gard sent her a glance. "Nice day for an outing."

"If it lasts," she said frostily.

"We can hope." He gave her another brief glance. She was wearing jeans, sneakers, and a short-sleeved, blue T-shirt. "Did you bring a jacket, just in case?"

"I grew up in Montana, remember? Yes, I brought a jacket." She had also brought her art supplies, which would give her something else to do beside bat at mosquitoes.

"You said you hated camping. I wonder why that is."

Her expression took on a slight smirk. "I think I explained why yesterday. I don't like sleeping on the ground and in the open. I'm not particularly fond of dirt and insects and badly prepared food. I enjoy hot baths and indoor plumbing. Actually, the list is endless, and since I've committed to doing this, it would probably be best to avoid talking about it."

"Oh. Well, sure, if you prefer."

She gave him a dirty look for his congeniality. She didn't want him being congenial and cheerful. It was only an act, in the first place, and in the second... well, there had to be another reason, though in all fairness it was probably only her own bad mood.

Going camping with Gard Sterling was the most inane thing she had ever done. He was, after all, the closest thing to an enemy that she had. Certainly he'd been a thorn in her side since she was seventeen years old, never mind the years that she hadn't been near him.

Cass became aware of direction, especially when Gard took an old road leading to the mountains. "Is that where we'll be camping, in the mountains?" she asked brusquely.

"Nope. I've got a special place in mind, but we have to go through these mountains to get there."

Determined not to enjoy any part of this fiasco, even the spectacular scenery, Cass put her head back and closed her eyes. "I'm going to catch a nap. Wake me when we get there."

Gard glanced her way, saw her closed eyes and shook his head. Obviously she wasn't going to unbend easily. Patience was something he had gradually learned over the past few years, but to be honest his patience hadn't really been tested in quite a while. This week with Cass was going to test it plenty, he suspected.

In a few minutes he realized that she really had fallen asleep, because her head bounced when the road dipped or swelled. She probably hadn't slept very well last night, which was probably his fault. For several miles he sympathized with her. Her accusation of him railroading her was pretty damned accurate, and yes, he felt some guilt about it.

But she never would have returned to Montana otherwise. This camping trip was his final attempt to bring them together, he had already decided. If it didn't work he would give her the answer he'd promised and that would be the end of their relationship, business as well as personal, because he could only give her a no on buying the Whitfield property. The only way he could buy her ranch was to go into debt up to his eyeballs, which he didn't want to do. So in two weeks she would be putting her land on the market and God only knew who his new neighbor would be.

Gard's lips thinned at the thought. Nothing would ever be the same again, would it? His parents gone. Cass's parents gone. Cass out of his life?

He inhaled a long, painful breath and released it slowly, all the time keeping his eyes on the road. This week *had* to work. If it didn't...

No, he wouldn't think of that now. He had to keep an upbeat, positive attitude. For one thing, the place he was taking Cass wasn't your everyday camping spot. She was bound to be impressed and might even like it.

But what he really wanted to happen was for her to like him. Or, better still, admit that she had always liked him, even if he had been a horse's rear end in his wild and woolly youth.

Heaving a somewhat confused sigh, Gard made a right turn onto another road. They were still in the mountains, still ascending. There were several more turns, each road becoming a little cruder than its predecessor. And finally he reached the summit of one particular mountain and the road started down.

It kept going down and getting rougher and less delineated until they had reached the floor of a small, secluded valley. Then the road petered out completely. Driving slowly over uneven, grassy ground for another mile or so, Gard reached his destination. He stopped the truck and turned off the engine.

He looked at his sleeping companion. "Cass? We're here."

Her eyelids fluttered as she came awake. "What?"

"We're here."

It took a few seconds for her to get her bearings. Then she remembered who she was with and why she had a crick in her neck. Rubbing the stiffness in her neck, she looked out the windows then blinked in surprise. They were in a beautiful spot, only a few feet away from a small, sparkling pond of water. Next she took in the ledges of almost-white rock to the left of the pond, and the steam rising from several pools. The foliage was a vivid green, thick and lush in places. And surrounding the little valley, rising like the most stately of sentinels, were the mountains, purple and blue and green, with the very highest still bearing patches of last winter's snow.

"Where are we?" she asked, utterly amazed that this incredible place was within driving distance of where she had grown up and she hadn't even heard about it, let alone seen it.

Gard was looking out the windows, as well. "It doesn't have a name that I know of. I've never seen another person out here, so I'm not sure that anyone else even knows about it."

"The forest service must," Cass murmured, awestruck by the beauty everywhere she looked.

"Maybe so, but so far the government hasn't attempted to control its usage." He looked at her with a hint of a smile. "Ready to get out?"

"Are those hot springs I see over there?" Cass asked as she opened her door and slid to the ground.

"Sure are. And they drain off into the lake, which keeps it at a nice swimming temperature during the summer months." Gard jumped out.

"It's not much good for fishing, though, I'll bet."

"No, it's not. But there's a great trout stream at the other end of the valley, about a half-mile hike from here."

Cass was looking at the mountains, turning slowly in a full circle. "They're gorgeous from here," she said softly, as though speaking to herself.

"Go on," Gard urged. "Explore. Get yourself acquainted with the place. I'll unload the truck and set up camp."

Cass stopped looking at the scenery to look at him. "I'd offer to help, but I know next to nothing about camping gear."

"I don't need any help. Relax. Enjoy yourself. I'll have everything taken care of in no time."

Cass nodded and began wandering off. She turned around and called, "Did your father show you this place?"

Gard was untying the tarp. "I found it on my own," he called back.

She had been thinking that this might have been one of the places Ridge Whitfield and Loyal Sterling had enjoyed together, but probably not if Loyal hadn't taken his son here. Then again, she amended, had Loyal and his son done *any* camping or fishing together? The youthful Gard in her memory hadn't put his time in fishing, not unless it included a tub of iced-down beer and girls in short-shorts.

That was pure conjecture, of course. Cass had no first-hand knowledge of Gard's activities in those days, and was basing her opinion on rumor, gossip, and the occasional glimpse she'd gotten of him in the midst of one rowdy event or another.

Until that night at the dunes, of course, when her first-hand knowledge had suddenly jumped off the scale.

Walking to the water's edge—she had thought the word *pond,* but Gard had called it a lake—Cass bent down and got her hand wet. The water was warm and silky, and she wished she had packed a bathing suit. But the possibility of swimming during the dreadful week simply hadn't occurred to her.

Rising, her gaze swept the view again. Maybe the week wouldn't be so dreadful, after all. This was an incredible place, peaceful and beautiful to the eye. The fly in the ointment, of course, was being here with Gard.

Gard unloaded the truck and began the job of setting up camp. Every so often he would look around for Cass and find her in various locations well within sight. The hot pools fascinated her, apparently, because she spent quite a lot of time walking among them and testing the water temperature.

Because the sun had reached the high, hot point of the day and the mountains buffered most of the breezes passing through the area, Gard was soon sweating. Removing his shirt, he tossed it over the fender of his truck and returned to work.

Cass was sitting on an expanse of white rock near one of the pools when she glanced over at Gard and saw the sun glistening on his darkly tanned torso. Her eyes narrowed in intense appreciation of the marvelous lines of his body. Did she even know another man built so well as Gard? From an artist's point of view, he would make a wonderful model, muscular in his shoulders, arms and legs, and lean in the middle. Just about perfect, she thought with a burst of resentment. He always had been perfect in the looks department, and even when he got old and gray his looks would probably still be titillating women. Damned man.

Well, he was doing all the work, and maybe she should let him. But she had her own things to look after and it wouldn't kill her to help out a little.

Standing, she dusted off the seat of her jeans and ambled toward the campsite. One tent was already up and sturdy and Gard was working on a second. Gard saw her approaching.

"That first tent is yours. I've fixed your bed and put your luggage inside. Take a look and see if it's all right."

It was a large tent, tall enough for Cass to walk into without stooping. She did a double take over the bed. Kneeling to examine it at closer range, she discovered a thick air mattress, a two-inch padding of foam rubber, and finally, a large sleeping bag that contained clean white sheets and a soft pillow.

She sat back on her heels. This was nothing like the camping trip her father had taken her on. Then, her sleeping bag had been on the ground and in the open. All night long, she remembered, she had worried about some spider or insect dropping from the pine trees under which they were sleeping onto her face.

Why, this tent even had a window! Scrambling to her feet, Cass unzipped the square of canvas and permitted the daylight to come through the plastic window.

Gard appeared in the doorway. "What do you think?"

"I think..." she began excitedly. *Hold it,* she chided herself. *You don't need to gush all over the place just because you won't have to worry about spiders in your face at night.* "It will do," she finished with very little emotion.

"Good." He turned to go.

"Uh, there must be something I can do, even if I don't understand the fine art of putting up tents."

Her offer gave Gard a good feeling. She'd warm up and lose that pinched-mouth expression before this week was over. He would bet on it.

"Thanks. Come on out and I'll show you the kitchen."

"The kitchen? Really, now..." But she followed him out and then stood with her mouth open while he showed her not only a propane gas stove but a gas refrigerator. It was small, to be sure, but amazing.

"I've started the refrigerator, so it should be getting cold. If you'd like, you can take the food from the ice chest and put it in the fridge," Gard said. "The other food will stay in those metal boxes."

Cass was long finished with the food organization before Gard was through setting up camp. They had a folding table and two chairs, and the tarp that had covered the load in his pickup had been hoisted onto four sturdy poles to provide shade over the kitchen and dining area.

This was first-class camping, Cass had to admit, if only to herself. Good food, a great bed, a tent to bathe and change clothes in, and the most fabulous array of scenery she had ever seen. She would have to look long and hard to find something to gripe about, she realized. Gard had even thought of their necessary bodily functions, which she certainly hadn't wanted to bring up.

He gave her a small shovel and a roll of toilet tissue. "When we leave here, this place will be exactly as we found it. Your bathroom is to the left, mine is to the right. Everything is buried. Understand?"

"Yes," she said, wondering when he had become so tactful that he could get such a personal point across without embarrassing her.

Finally he stood with his hands on his hips and surveyed the campsite with a satisfied expression. "It's done." He was dirty and sweaty, and he eyed the lake. "I'm going for a dip. Care to join me?"

"I didn't bring a bathing suit," she said stiffly, hoping he got the point that he could have said something about bringing one along.

"Neither did I," he replied evenly, and started walking toward the lake.

Wide-eyed, Cass watched. Was he going in with his jeans on? He wouldn't dare get naked, would he?

Indeed he would dare, she soon realized. He kicked off his boots, took off his socks, dropped his jeans and briefs on the ground and waded into the water. All she saw was his backside, but her pulse was suddenly racing like the wind.

Ignoring that unnerving reaction, she sat on a chair and folded her arms. If he thought skinny-dipping was on *her* agenda for the week, he had another think coming.

But darn, it looked like fun. He was cavorting in the water like a kid, swimming a few strokes, then diving below the surface. She knew how warm the water was and watched Gard enviously, wondering at the same time just how much she should allow herself to enjoy this forced outing. Wouldn't it be terribly traitorous to her own self to just let go and have fun, considering how sneakily Gard had pressured her into coming?

Watching Gard, a sudden fear struck her. It was all about feelings, and it was unexpected and startling. Ever since their initial meeting at the Plantation, she had been trying with all her might to hang on to those old hurts. True, she had slipped badly the night Gard had come along when she'd been crying at the dunes, but as soon as she had regained some common sense, she had also regained the resentment she had lived with for fourteen years.

But something else had happened since their reunion, and this was the first time she had acknowledged it. Her feelings for Gard no longer consisted exclusively of resentment and dislike. In fact, they were dangerously close to—

No! She wouldn't permit it! Getting to her feet, Cass turned her back on the lake and began walking. There were several groves of trees nearby and she headed for one to hide her teary eyes. She was *not* going to fall in love with Rebel Sterling again, she wasn't!

Nine

When Cass returned to camp Gard was dressed and making sandwiches. He sent her a glance. "Hungry?"

"A little."

They ate standing around, rather than using the table and chairs. Cass just wasn't in the mood for the camaraderie of a sit-down meal, and eating this way seemed to keep them more distanced than using the table would have.

Gard caught on, but acted as though eating sandwiches and drinking lemonade on their feet was perfectly normal. He wondered what subjects he could introduce for conversation that wouldn't cause a negative reaction in Cass. It hadn't surprised him that she had disappeared when he came out of the lake, but he'd honestly thought she had merely stepped into her tent to avoid his nudity. She could have done the same thing by turning her back, and she had done neither. She had gone for a walk, apparently. She definitely was not in a friendly mood, so he chose his words carefully.

"Great weather," he murmured between bites, his gaze on the scenery. "You know, those hot pools are terrific. You'll have to give them a try. The lake, too, Cass."

"Yeah, right."

Her sarcasm wasn't lost on Gard. "You could go in wearing a pair of shorts or something, couldn't you?"

Of course she could. For that matter, she could get wet in a pair of jeans. After all, there wasn't a law against swimming or sitting in a hot pool fully clothed, if that was what one preferred.

But doing those things would make Gard think her resentment was relenting, and Cass wasn't sure she wanted to be that kind. She was here under duress, and just maybe he should be kept aware of that.

Besides, a new worry was nagging Cass. As ridiculous as it was, some adolescent part of herself kept remembering Gard's potent lovemaking, and they were going to be out here for seven days and nights. There had to be a solid, unbreachable line drawn between them, and as he had no qualms about taking off his clothes right in front of her, it was up to her to keep things rational.

Cass finished her lemonade. "Lunch was good. Thanks," she said, sounding polite but indifferent.

Gard refused to be baited by her tone. "You're welcome. I think I'll take in a little fishing. Would you like to go along? If we're lucky, we'll have fresh trout for dinner."

"Fishing?" Cass's nose wrinkled in distaste. "No, I don't think so. I'll just stick around here. You go ahead, though."

"I'll probably be gone a couple of hours."

"No problem. I might do some sketching." Occasionally she did a landscape, though it had been quite a while since her last. But this place appealed to her creativity. Aroused it, to be factual. She wasn't ready to haul out her oils and canvases, but a little sketching might bring some ideas to light.

Gard gathered his fishing gear. "Are you sure you won't mind being here alone?"

"Positive," she said dryly. The more time they spent apart, he involved with his activities, she with hers, the easier the week would be. It still seemed impossible that she was out here at all, blackmailed into a week of camping. Did he honestly think she would give him the satisfaction of relaxing and enjoying herself?

Well, she might enjoy herself a little during his absences. May they be many, she thought spitefully as he walked away from camp. This place really was incredibly beautiful and hard not to enjoy. Her gaze swept the panorama of mountains, miniature lake, lush foliage and natural hot pools. Yes, most definitely it was a beautiful spot. Certainly one could never capture its special essence in tones of charcoal, or at least, she couldn't. She needed color to really express herself in art, but a few sketches in charcoal to get the feeling of the area in her system wouldn't hurt.

Cass went into her tent for a pad and her pencils.

There was a nice fire burning in the fire pit Gard had constructed by scooping out some earth and ringing the hole with rocks. Other than the stars overhead, the fire was the only light in sight. They sat near the fire, Cass on a log, Gard on the ground. Dinner had been the trout he'd caught and it had been delicious, but the atmosphere had been strained and they had eaten rather silently.

He wanted to get Cass talking, somehow alter her attitude and make her smile. After adding another chunk of wood to the fire, he sat down again.

"The day I stumbled across this valley, it was pouring rain," he said.

"Oh?"

"I was hunting. Deer season. Driving the backroads, following some I'd never been on before. Finding this place was pure accident. I remember seeing the steam rising from the hot pools and thinking it was fog. But it really didn't look like any fog I'd ever seen before. I drove into the valley as far as I could and parked right about where the truck is now. Then I got out and walked over to the pools. There are hot springs north of Huntington, but I'd never heard of any out this way. I spent about an hour looking around and decided to come back when the sun was out."

"You must have gotten soaked." It was said wryly, as though he didn't have sense enough to stay out of the rain.

Gard ignored her tone. "I was dressed for it. Even so, I got a little wet. Anyway, I did come back, and I really liked the place."

Cass liked it, too, but she wasn't about to say so. In fact, sitting in the dark with the fire reflecting on his handsome face, she had to reinforce her resolve to remain unaffected by anything he said or did this week.

They were so alone out there, and the night quiet, broken only by the crackling of the fire, was discomfiting. And yet she couldn't stop herself from looking at him, and remembering herself lying on the trunk of her own car, remembering him holding her hips while he...

She drew an unsteady breath and suddenly wanted to hurt him, to shake his macho confidence. "Do you ever think of the past?" she asked. "Those days when you said to hell with the rest of the world and jumped headlong into anything that came to your mind, no matter how it might affect other people?"

Gard's eyes narrowed slightly. "I think of it." After a minute he added, "What I can remember of it. I still don't remember that night at the dunes with you."

She winced. "You didn't have to say that. I already knew it."

Gard picked up a long stick and poked at the fire with it. "But I remember every moment of our second time."

"You didn't have to say that, either," she said sharply. "Not when it's something *I'm* trying to forget."

He laughed without humor. "You're not going to forget it, any more than I am." The stick stopped moving as he peered at her across the fire. "Why do you want to forget?"

"Why?" she repeated with exaggerated incredulity. "Why would I want to remember?"

"I could understand if you hadn't liked it, but..."

"What makes you so sure I liked it? God, the ego of some men. And please don't say that you can tell when a woman likes it. That's plain bull. All men know for certain are their own feelings. They have no idea what a woman feels during sex."

Gard laughed again, this time sounding disbelieving. "You're dead wrong, honey. If all a woman does is lie there like a stick, which I've heard some do, then a man knows she isn't enjoying the act, right? But when she moves and moans the way you did that night..."

"Oh, stop," Cass said abruptly. "Do you think I need a reminder of every stupid thing I did?"

"You know, that's the second time you called yourself stupid for making love with me. Do you think every woman who responds to a man does so out of stupidity? Maybe you think making love is stupid in itself. Is that it?"

"Making love should be confined to two people in love."

"Oh, I see. You should be in love before you *make* love. Well, the world might be a calmer, more serene place if that's the way it was, but I doubt if there's much you or I could do to alter centuries-old attitudes. Sex is an instinctive, natural function of every living thing."

"You're wrong. Procreation is what's instinctive. Humans are the only species who have sex strictly for pleasure." Why in God's name was she discussing sex with Gard? "Let's change the subject," she said flatly.

"But I like this one." He spoke with laughter in his voice.

"You would."

"You would, too, if you weren't so hung up on the past."

"Don't psychoanalyze me, Gard."

"Psychoanalyze a woman? God forbid. What ordinary man could even begin to understand women, let alone probe their psyche?"

"My point, exactly."

"But that works two ways, my dear," he said with deep-voiced melodrama, waggling his eyebrows at the same time.

"Oh, for pity's sake," Cass said disgustedly.

"Are you telling me that you understand men?"

"Yes, actually, I am."

"You understand me."

She smirked. "A whole lot more than you think."

"Interesting. Very interesting," Gard murmured softly. "Do you know what's going through my mind right now?"

"Pretty much, yes."

"Wonderful! Will you do it with me?"

Cass stared, then turned red. "You are, without a doubt, the crudest individual I've ever known."

"Hey, didn't you just say you knew what I was thinking? What's crude about asking you to take a dip in one of those hot pools with me?"

"That's *not* what you were asking me!"

"Sorry, babe, but it was."

Furious and embarrassed, Cass got to her feet. "I hope you drown. Good night." His laughter followed her into her tent, where she located the flashlight and used it to see to strike a match and light the lantern. Her hands were far from steady and she felt like bawling. Quickly she got out of her clothes and into a nightgown. Then, crawling into her bed, she turned down the lantern until the flame died. She was still trembling. "I hate you," she whispered in the dark.

But it was the biggest lie she had ever told herself. That was the problem. She wanted to hate Gard with every fiber of her being and she didn't. It wasn't fair.

Gard took his soak in the hottest pool, looking up at the stars while he thought of Cass. She was so set against him that maybe this week *wouldn't* do any good. Obviously she hated being pushed, and he had pushed her hard.

But how else would he have gotten her to return to Montana? As for forcing her into taking this camping trip, he'd had to do something. One look at her face at the airport had told him that she wasn't going to be receptive to an ordinary courtship.

Well, this wasn't ordinary and one might even find it difficult to label it a courtship. But that was what it was to him. Now all he had to do was get Cass to relax.

Yeah, he thought sardonically. That was all he had to do.

How?

Cass awoke groaning. Her heart was pounding. She had kicked her legs loose from the sheets and sleeping bag, and her skin was damp with perspiration. The dream... the dream... What was it? A man, yes. A stranger. Or no, not a stranger, just someone she couldn't identify.

The dream slipped into her subconscious, leaving a residue of discomfort and anxiety. Sitting up, Cass massaged her temples with her fingertips. The total darkness of the tent felt smothering. Crawling to the flap, she pushed it open and breathed deeply of the cool night air.

Remnants of the dream returned. A man... touching her... advancing and retreating. She hated dreams that weren't distinctly recalled and yet were so disturbing. Probably everyone had them at one time or another. She hadn't kept score, but there had been a few over the years that still bothered her when she thought of them. This one was particularly unnerving.

She had bought a book on dreams one time, and according to its author everything one dreamed, or practically everything, was symbolic of something else. So she had learned that dreaming of a white horse meant good luck, and a dream about death had about a dozen different connotations. Some of the symbolism had made sense, some of it hadn't.

But what about the dreams a person couldn't remember and that created terrible confusion? What did they symbolize? Did she believe any of it, anyway? She had probably given that book away, because she was sure it wasn't in the cliff house with her others.

She was suddenly terribly thirsty and felt around until she found the flashlight. Gard had brought along three five-gallon containers—equipped with spigots—of drinking water, and reaching one of them was all she could think of.

Stepping out of the tent, she flashed the light around the campsite. The fire in the pit was long dead, she saw. What time was it?

Making her way to the water cans, she looked for something to drink out of and grabbed a cup off of the table that one of them, either Gard or she, had used for coffee after dinner. She really didn't care whose cup it had been. Setting down the flashlight with the light beamed on the spigot, she filled the cup and emptied it without taking a breath.

The night coolness felt good on her feverish skin, and she filled a second cup, picked up the flashlight and sat down in one of the chairs. Realizing then that the moon had risen and the area really wasn't that dark, she switched off the flashlight.

Sipping the second cup of water, she sat there and tried to recapture that elusive dream.

"Is something wrong?"

Cass jumped. "Oh! You startled me. Sorry I woke you. I needed a drink of water."

Gard moved around Cass's chair to take the other one. He leaned forward, toward her. "It's all right. I sleep light when I'm not in my own bed." He paused. "Were you having trouble sleeping?" Her nightgown wasn't revealing, but her arms were bare and her hair was appealingly disheveled. She was beautiful in the moonlight, he thought, taking a deliberately cautious breath so she wouldn't catch on that he was physically affected by this unexpected middle-of-the-night encounter.

"No, I slept very well. But..."

Gard waited a moment, but when she didn't say more, he asked, "Did something wake you, then? A sound?"

Cass hesitated another moment, uncertain about talking with Gard about that dream. She still felt its troubling aftermath. But she had to give him some kind of answer. "It was a dream," she finally said reluctantly.

"A nightmare?"

"No, just one of those vague dreams that leave you feeling a little discombobulated." She raised the cup to her lips and for the first time realized that Gard had pulled on jeans and nothing else. Averting her eyes from his naked chest, she added, "Then I needed a drink of water. It was nothing, really, and I'm sorry I woke you."

"Like I said, I'm a light sleeper." His eyes lifted to the sky. "Look at that moon, would you?"

"Yes, it's beautiful. I was using the flashlight, but then I realized it wasn't needed."

"It's not as beautiful as you are, Cass," he said softly. "Nothing is."

Her gaze slowly swung around to him. "I don't want you saying things like that."

"But it's true."

"Of course it's not true. It's flattery, pure and simple. It's an attempt to...to soften my attitude toward this whole business."

"It's not flattery, Cass. It's how I feel."

Why didn't she just get up and return to her tent? She didn't have to sit there and talk nonsense with him.

But something was holding her in that chair, maybe the gorgeous moon, maybe the cool, night air.

Maybe it was simply being with another person in this isolated valley after a disturbing dream, or maybe it was because that person was Gard. Cass took another swallow of water, nervous suddenly. "I wonder what time it is."

"About midnight."

"The witching hour," Cass murmured. Was Gard the man in that dream? The man who had appeared and disappeared and left her feeling so empty and unsettled?

"Any hour with you is bewitching," Gard said, speaking softly.

"I said 'witching,' not *be*witching."

"In either case, you've cast a spell over me."

"That's silly."

Gard scooted his chair closer to hers, until their knees were almost touching. Cass felt a moment of panic. If he made a pass now, when she was feeling so vulnerable and alone, she might not be able to maintain the hands-off attitude she'd been so determined to sustain. She felt especially crowded when he leaned forward again and put his hands on the arms of her chair.

"Gard . . . no," she said tremulously.

"No, what? I haven't done anything."

"You're working up to it," she accused.

"Cass . . . I can't stop thinking of you," he said, his voice husky with emotion. "If you know a way to stop one's thoughts, tell me about it."

She looked away, recalling those awful months after their first time at the dunes, when all she'd been able to think of was him. "I'm not the one to ask," she said in a near whisper.

"You've had the same experience? With who, Cass?" He held his breath, praying she would say, *With you.*

"It was a long time ago and I have no intention of talking about it." She sucked in a much-needed breath. The conversation was approaching dangerous territory, making her very uneasy. "I think I'll go back to bed now, if you'd be kind enough to move your chair so I can get up."

"Cass . . . please talk about it," Gard pleaded. It *was* him she had referred to, he was sure of it. Because of their intertwined past, brief as it had been.

Or was that merely wishful thinking? Maybe it was his ego directing his thoughts. Dare he forget their meeting at the Plantation, when she sure hadn't acted as though she was glad to see him? If only she would open up with him.

"Cass, stay and talk to me. Just for a while longer."

She found herself staring into his eyes, which looked black in the moonlight, black and penetrating and impassioned. In the pit of her stomach was the thing she feared, an overwhelming reaction to his sexual potency, his masculine power. She had to put a stop to this, here and now.

"There's been too much animosity over that old contract for us to ever be friends," she said with all the calmness she could muster.

"Friends?" Gard almost laughed, though it wouldn't have been from amusement.

"Well, that's what you said, isn't it? That you wanted us to become friends?"

"You know damned well I meant more," he retorted, taking the cup from her hand and setting it on the ground before she could react. Then he clasped both of her hands in his. She tried to pull them back, but he held on. "I want you, and you know it, too, don't you?"

"I know nothing of the kind. Let go of my hands." Her heart was hammering in her chest, making her voice breathy and not very strong.

Instead of complying, he bent forward, buried his face in the curve of her throat and inhaled. "You smell like heaven must. Like flowers... and honey... and sunshine."

"Gard...stop," she moaned. "I knew you were going to do something like this, I just knew it."

"That's what I just said, sweetheart. You know that I want you."

"That's not what I meant!"

"Sure it is." Still holding her hands, he raised his head, looking into her eyes from about four inches away. "You don't hate me anymore, do you, Cass?"

She released a heavy sigh. "I never hated you. But I don't want an affair with you, either."

He brought her hands up to his lips. "I think you do," he said softly, breathing on her fingers. "I think you ache for me, just like I ache for you."

"Think again, Gard."

"I have. A hundred times, a thousand, and it always comes out the same. That night at the dunes proved something, Cass. Nothing could have stopped us from making love. The sky could have fallen and we wouldn't have known it."

"And the first time?" she said coldly. "Would you have known if the sky fell in that time? You don't even remember the first time."

"And you can't get over that, can you? Honey..."

"Please stop. I'm exhausted and getting chilled."

"Come to my tent and let me warm you up," he whispered. "Let me hold you. Let me make love to you."

She swallowed hard. The picture he'd painted was much too appealing. "No...I...can't."

"Cass, you can do anything you want to do."

"No, that's the way *you* live, Gard, not me. Now, please let go of my hands. I want to go to bed."

"So do I, babe."

"Yes, but I want to go to bed alone."

"No, you don't. But..." Sighing, he released her hands and pushed his chair back. "Guess you're not ready yet."

Cass stumbled to her feet, suddenly angry. His remark had sounded smug and egotistical, as though he was just so positive that she would be "ready" before the week was up.

"Your ego astounds me," she threw at him. "Well, let me tell you what I think of a man who lies and connives to satisfy his lust. You are without a doubt—"

"I don't want to hear it." Snaking an arm out, Gard caught her around the waist and yanked her forward. His quickness took her by surprise and she fell against him. Before she could regain her balance his arms were around her and her face was pressed into his naked chest.

"Damn you," she cried, struggling to get free.

Somehow he managed to tip up her chin, and then, almost as easily, to press his lips to hers. His strength was ten times hers, twenty times, and fighting him did nothing but rub their bodies together.

She stopped fighting him because it was only making matters worse. His mouth opened on hers and he kissed her possessively, passionately.

Then he stopped kissing her and looked into her eyes. "It's going to happen, Cass. Maybe not tonight, maybe not tomorrow, but it is going to happen."

"When I'm ready," she said with heavy sarcasm, though it was an effort to belittle his opinion when she was weak from the yearning in her own body. "Do you think I'm suddenly going to announce, 'Hey, Gard, I'm ready'?"

"Something like that. We'll both know." He dropped his arms and took a backward step. "Good night, Sassy Cassie," he said softly. "If you have another bad dream, come to my tent and I'll chase all the bogeymen away."

"Fat chance." Trembling, she turned and headed for her own tent. Crawling into her sleeping bag, she huddled into a ball and squeezed her eyes shut.

Vowing to stay distanced from Gard was one thing; doing it was quite another.

It was a long time before she fell back to sleep.

Ten

Cass's eyes opened to daylight, and her first thought was of the inanity of this camping trip. Disgust made her feel suddenly weak. She had sworn to never go camping again with her very own father, for hell's sake, and here she was doing it with a man she didn't even trust. Now she had to get up and face Gard, and figure out the best way to take a bath, and then try to fill a long day while avoiding any more sexual shenanigans as had occurred in the night. A week of this would have her tearing out her hair.

Maybe if she feigned illness, Gard would take her home. *Gard, I think I'm coming down with a bug.* Cass grimaced. He wasn't apt to accept her diagnosis without a few questions. *Do you have a fever? Are you feeling nauseous?* And she would have to elaborate on the lie, when she had never been very good at lying. Besides, if he caught on, he might cancel their agreement and she wanted that buy/sell option settled. She was going to have to see this fiasco through, like it or not.

Listening, she could detect no sounds or movements beyond the tent, which indicated to her that Gard was still sleeping. It felt early. Cass had laid her watch on the tent floor at the head of her bed last night, a safe enough place, she'd figured. Reaching for it, she checked the time and saw that it was eight, not nearly as early as she'd thought.

But she was in no hurry to get up and begin what could only be another discomfiting day. Lying there, her mind wandered, and it was no surprise to her that it wandered clear back to her teens, when she had been so crazy about Gard "Rebel" Sterling that she had lived and breathed for the mere sight of him. Those days were special. Closing her eyes, Cass could almost see him on his motorcycle, wearing his customary tight jeans and black leather jacket. At once she felt the tremors of desire in the pit of her stomach.

"Damn," she whispered, shaken that a mere memory had so much power over her senses.

Life had been much less complex during those days of motorcycles and black leather jackets, she decided. Not that her crush on Gard had been all that simple. She had suffered over him as only a teenager can suffer, but she had been able to focus on her own small world without the many ifs, ands and buts badgering her these days.

Her world had broadened as she had grown up, of course, which was only normal. But desiring Gard now was so complicated she might never sort it out. They were adults and she was beyond mere crushes. Besides, did she even *like* Gard? Look at all of the trouble he had caused her. And another thing, she didn't doubt that he would take her to bed in a minute, but despite his statements to the contrary, dare she believe that he wouldn't do the same with any reasonably attractive woman?

Cass let go of a heavy, put-upon sigh, then forced herself off the low bed and to her feet. She probably had only herself to blame for being here, what with her impatience to get the ranch sold.

Frowning, Cass slowly sank back down to the bed. For the first time since her decision to sell, she felt a pang of guilt about it. Ridge Whitfield had loved his ranch, and though he had accepted Cass's preference to live in Oregon, she would bet it had never occurred to him that she would do her level best to turn the Whitfield Land and Cattle Company into cash only months after his death. Would he have been hurt by her indifference to the place he'd loved most in the world?

It wasn't that she was indifferent, Cass mentally and uneasily argued in self-defense. It was just that her future wasn't in Montana.

But that defense, reasonable though it was, didn't quieten the guilt, which seemed to be getting stronger.

Oh, this is just great, she thought, distressed that guilt would start haranguing her at this point. Until this very moment her plans had been bolstered by confidence. Why, all of a sudden, was she uncertain about something of which she'd been only positive?

Disturbed by so much unexpected ambiguity, she stood again and moved to open the tent flap enough to peer out. The bright sunlight made her blink, but she looked around the campsite with Gard in mind. Was he in his tent, or what?

Gingerly she stepped outside and was immediately stopped by one of the folding chairs, placed in a conspicuous spot, apparently so she wouldn't miss the piece of paper lying on its seat and held down by a bar of soap and a tube of shampoo.

Cass picked up all three, the soap, the shampoo and the paper, which was a note from Gard.

Cass,

I'm going for a hike. Feel free to use the lake or any of the hot pools for a bath, but use this soap and shampoo, as they're made with special ingredients that won't damage the ecology of the water. I'll be back around nine and we'll have breakfast.

Gard

"Hmm," Cass murmured. At least she no longer had to worry about her morning bath, but the question was, had Gard foreseen some possible discomfort for her in the situation and deliberately gone off to alleviate it? Was he that farsighted? That considerate?

Examining the shampoo tube, she read that it, indeed, was recommended for use in fragile environments. From what she'd seen so far out here, Gard truly did plan to leave this lovely place in as pristine a condition as they had found it. She had to admire his respect for nature, but just how much respect did he have for her?

Sighing, Cass went back into her tent to exchange her nightgown for a robe and slippers. Carrying several towels, the soap and shampoo, she headed for the lake.

Gard was coming down a hill, making his way through the trees, when he spotted Cass dropping her robe and walking into the lake. She was a long way off, but not so far that he couldn't see her extremely nice body and long legs. Without the slightest qualm, he sat down to watch her bathe.

He'd been hiking since six-thirty and was ravenously hungry. Finally on his way back to camp, he'd been thinking that Cass would have finished with her morning routines, whatever they were, long before this. Apparently not. She must have slept in.

He took off his dark glasses to get a clearer view. Cass was standing in water up to her waist, shampooing her hair. "Beautiful," he said under his breath, meaning it heart and soul. He cared too much for Cass for his feelings to be a passing fancy, he realized again. He wanted this lady in his future. He wanted her in Montana, permanently. He wanted...

Frowning, he absently rubbed his jaw while he tried to understand his feelings. And Cass's. She had made passionate, uninhibited love with him, which had to mean something. That old contract sure had caused them a lot of problems, he thought. Why hadn't he told her the truth of his financial situation at their first meeting? Then maybe there wouldn't be a chasm between them.

But, no, that wasn't the real problem. Cass had arrived at that meeting with a bad taste in her mouth, because of what had happened between them years ago. Because they'd had a romantic interlude at the sand dunes in their youth, and…

And what? Why had she been there? Why had *he* been there? Even though there were a lot of foggy areas in his mind about those days, he felt certain they hadn't been dating. Only Cass knew the whole story, and she wasn't talking.

His eyes narrowed in speculation. Even if they had run into each other by accident at the dunes that long-ago night, why had she permitted intimacy? Yes, she had all but accused him of force, but then she had apologized for giving him that impression, which indicated to him that she had been a willing participant.

What had come after? Damn his faulty memory! This was something he *needed* to remember.

And then a brand-new idea startled him. Had Cass liked him back then, enough to make love with him at their first opportunity? Had she had a serious crush on Rebel Sterling that he hadn't been aware of? Wouldn't that explain her seemingly permanent resentment? It would hurt any woman to feel that she had finally gotten a man's attention and then have nothing come of it, wouldn't it?

A knot of nervous excitement churned in Gard's gut. That was it, wasn't it? Cass had liked him and he hadn't reciprocated—other than taking advantage of her affection for him one night at the dunes. No wonder she had walked into the Plantation's banquet room with a chip on her shoulder.

Gard sat back, pondering this new theory. Until this minute he hadn't considered that Cass might have had special feelings for him in their youth. If it was true, then those feelings had been for the wild, reckless young man he'd been in those days. Maybe it was the wildness, the recklessness that had appealed to her.

The changes in himself, which he'd been so proud of, just might be a big turnoff for Cass these days. She still retained some of those special feelings or she never would have responded to him a few weeks back. Maybe he'd been going at this all wrong, trying to show her what a solid citizen he was now. Maybe what she wanted from him—if she wanted anything at all—was some of his old wildness, his old cockiness.

He was still only speculating...but wasn't it worth a try? He'd do almost anything to break through that tough coat of armor with which Cass guarded her inner self, and maybe, just maybe, he had hit on the method.

Down at the lake, Cass waded from the water, wrapped her wet hair in one towel and dried off with the other. From his aerie in the trees, Gard watched with avid interest. He loved that woman. The thought made his mouth go dry, but it was the most profound truth he had ever stumbled upon.

Love. What a simple little word for the aching, driving passion in his body.

He got to his feet. It was time to start his new campaign with Sassy Cassie Whitfield.

All he could do was hope it worked.

Cass was dressed and drying her hair in the sun when she saw Gard returning. He must have gotten hot, because his shirt was tied around his waist rather than where it should be. Her lips thinned in self-rebuke. There wasn't a reason in the world for her to even notice his damned chest, or to think of sex at the sight of him. Didn't she have enough to worry about, what with her newly forged concerns about her hasty decision to sell the ranch? Actually, if she had changed her mind on selling, she could tell Gard to shove his decision up his nose.

But her mind wasn't that made up on that point yet. Watching Gard stride closer, she wondered if her interest in buying into the gallery was waning. She shook her head in disgust. She was getting more mixed up by the day, and whose fault was it? Without Gard dragging his heels, everything would already be done, or at least in the works.

"Hi, beautiful," Gard called from about fifty feet away.

She sent him an incredulous stare. Her clothing was a pair of baggy shorts and an oversize T-shirt. The only cosmetic on her face was some moisturizer, and her hair was still damp and snarled. Beautiful? Yeah, right.

"Hello," she said rather stiffly. Then she nearly fell off her chair trying to get up and out of his way. Laughing, he beat her to the punch by leaning over her and holding on to the arms of the chair, much as he'd done last night, effectively holding her in place.

"Get away from me," she said sharply. "What's wrong with you?"

"Nothing you can't cure, honey."

She glared into his eyes. "Don't look to me for any cures, buster."

Gard threw back his head and roared. At the same time he let go of her chair and backed up. Cass released a long-suffering sigh and rolled her eyes. What had put him in such a sunny mood?

"Well," Gard stated when he was through laughing, "what would you like for breakfast? Hey, I know. How about some best-in-the-West flapjacks?"

"Anything is fine," Cass said, casting him a wary glance. He was much too cheerful for her not to suspect some nefarious scheme percolating in his conniving brain.

Gard got busy preparing the flapjacks. "Let's see, we also need coffee and maybe some bacon. How does that sound?"

"I told you, anything is fine with me."

Gard grinned. "Anything goes, huh?"

"If we're still talking about breakfast, yes." She wished he would untie that damned shirt from around his waist and put it on. There was entirely too much masculine bare skin within the campsite for her to enjoy breakfast, even if it was "best-in-the-West" flapjacks.

Before he could do more than chuckle, Cass marched into her tent for her hairbrush. Grinning, Gard turned his attention to making breakfast. Cass was so easily riled by everything he did, she *had* to like him. Yes, indeedy, he'd finally figured out Miss Cassandra Whitfield.

They ate with very little conversation. Cass did relent enough to compliment his flapjacks, which were light and fluffy and delicious. She added, "I didn't know you could cook."

"Lots of things you don't know about me, babe." Gard finished off the coffee in his cup and sat back with an air of satisfaction. His stomach was full, he was alone with Cass, the day was glorious, and the area was beautiful and, yes, romantic.

"I wish you wouldn't call me 'babe,'" Cass said with a stony expression. "It's a sexist label and demeaning."

Gard's left eyebrow lifted. "Oh? Is 'honey' sexist and demeaning, too? How about 'sweetheart'?"

"Words such as those should only be used between lovers."

"We're lovers."

"We are not! One, uh, misstep does not make a pair of lovers."

"Two." Cass stared blankly. "Two missteps," Gard reminded her.

She tossed her head disdainfully. "You can hardly count the first time when you don't even remember it."

"But you remember it, so it counts. I think a simplified definition of the word *lovers* is two people making love. That's what we did, sweetheart, make love. Conclusion... we're lovers."

"Are you purposely trying to irritate me this morning?" Cass looked irritated, all right.

"Wouldn't dream of it."

She glared at him. "You're so damned smug, it's sickening. You and I are *not* lovers, and your definition is...is stupid. So is your conclusion."

Gard chuckled. "Okay, tell me your definition of the word."

"As I said only last night, lovers are people *in* love," Cass snapped. "You and I are not in love."

His eyes narrowed on her. "Do you know that to be fact?"

"Well, I know *I'm* not in love!" Cass got up from her chair. "That's the end of this conversation as far as I'm concerned. I'm going to do the dishes."

"You are? Hey, that's really nice of you. But I've got a better idea. We'll do them together."

"Great," Cass muttered. "Look, why don't you find something else to do and let me take care of these few dishes by myself?"

"By any chance, could you be trying to get rid of me?" he asked teasingly, getting to his feet.

"I think that's an impossibility. You're a lot like flypaper."

Gard laughed. "Does that make you the fly?"

"That makes me an idiot." She put her hands on her hips. "I think we need to strike a deal. You cook and I'll clean up. Or I'll cook and *you* clean up. This kitchen isn't big enough for both of us."

The "kitchen" was wide open and couldn't be less confining. If one wanted to exaggerate, it could take in the whole valley.

"Well," Gard said with an injured expression, "I guess I know when I'm not wanted."

"Now you've got the idea," Cass said frostily. She turned to look at the neatly arranged boxes nearby, thinking that one of them had to contain a dishpan and some soap. Last night she hadn't offered to help with the dishes, and in fact had taken a walk around the lake while Gard did them, so she really didn't know where he kept the necessary items.

But afterward she'd felt a little guilty about leaving him with all the work and had decided to do her share in this miserable arrangement. Not together, though. Either she was going to do the dishes or he was, and if he didn't stop arguing about it, it was going to be him.

She let out a yelp when she felt Gard's arms come around her and pull her back against him. "What the hell are you doing?"

"Proving that we're still lovers," he whispered, nuzzling the side of her neck.

"Gard, don't," she groaned, trying to pry his forearms loose from their grip around her.

"Baby, I have to." He moved his body against her backside.

She could feel the hard wall of chest on her shoulder blades and smell his musky maleness. "This is not proving a thing," she said, appalled that her voice would sound husky and sexy when she had meant to sound affronted.

"It's sure proving something to me."

"Only that you're male." She was no longer plucking at his forearms to get rid of them. Her head was lying back against his bare shoulder and her eyes were closed. Worst of all, her voice was oozing sexual hoarseness. "The dishes," she whispered in a feeble attempt to stop this foolishness.

"What dishes?" Gard breathed deeply, inhaling her clean, soapy scent. "Holding you makes me feel twenty years old again."

"How nice for you." She tried to sound sarcastic, but it didn't come off very well. The delicious languor spreading throughout her body seemed to be controlling even the inflections of her speech.

She sighed, keeping silent while her mind raced. Did she want an affair with Gard while she was in Montana? Apparently he did. But her "affairs" had been few and far between, and she had always felt in control of her emotions with other men. With Gard, everything was different; control was laughable and her emotions ran wild. Wasn't this a dangerous game for her to be playing?

Yes, she decided, again trying to extricate herself. "Let go of me!"

"Do you know what I'd like to do right now?" he whispered while nibbling her earlobe.

"I'm not totally dense," she muttered. "Of course I know."

"Is it all right with you?"

"No, it is not! Gard... damn you..." She dug her fingernails into his forearms, just above his wrists.

"Hey," he exclaimed. "Are you trying to draw blood?"

"It's a thought."

"Want to play rough, huh?" His grin was on full throttle, though Cass couldn't see it. "Suits me, babe." Without further ado, he moved fast and scooped her up into his arms.

Startled, she began kicking and squirming. "Put me down, you... you..."

He was walking, carrying her away from the tents. "Simmer down, or we'll both end up flat on our, uh, butts."

Cass was fuming. "Oh, if I only had the strength, I'd punch you so hard you'd see stars." She eyed the hot pools, which seemed to be Gard's destination. "What are you doing?"

"You'll see." He was getting a little winded. "How much do you weigh?"

"That's none of your damned business. I hope your stupid arms fall off."

"Then you'd end up on your butt for sure," he retorted with a laugh.

"You think this is funny, don't you?" The hot pools were getting closer. "If you throw me in one of those pools, I will not be responsible for the consequences."

"Meaning what? That you'll lie in wait for an opportunity to avenge my terrible deed?"

"You've been warned," she said as menacingly as she could.

Gard laughed again. "Fair enough."

He stopped at the edge of the hottest pool, then decided that might be too much of a shock for Cass and walked over to one with a lower temperature. "Here goes."

"Don't you dare!"

"Never could resist a dare, sweetheart." Chuckling, he threw her into the pool and immediately jumped in himself.

Cass came up sputtering. "You maniac!" She began pushing the hair out of her eyes. Rising to stand in the pool, Gard started laughing, which made Cass angrier than the dunking. "I thought you'd outgrown adolescent behavior," she said in a scathingly insulting tone. "Don't waste your breath on any more lies about watching sunsets and...and..." She paused to catch her own breath, then gave him a murderous look. "I hate and despise you."

"No, you don't. You only wish you did."

"What an astonishing ego," she drawled. Pulling her T-shirt away from her chest as Gard seemed unduly fascinated with its clinging fit, Cass started moving toward the edge of the pool. She couldn't believe it when he grabbed her from behind and hauled her underwater again.

This time she came up shrieking. "Are you completely off your rocker?" Furiously she wiped the hair from her face again. "This is exactly the sort of idiotic thing you were famous for in the old days. This and drinking yourself blind."

"If I was as bad as you say, how come you liked me?"

"Liked you! Where on earth did you get *that* idea?"

Gard leaned against the side of the pool. "Then you didn't like me?"

Cass sneered. "Finally he understands."

"If you didn't like me, how come you made love with me?"

She stared at his smiling face, turned beet red, then started for the opposite side of the pool. "You bastard. I'm getting out, and..." One did not run in a waist-deep hot pool, she angrily realized. Gard didn't even try to run. He dove, took her by the ankles and pulled her under. She could see his grin in the crystal-clear water, and she launched herself at him with the intention of inflicting bodily damage in some shape or form.

They wrestled underwater for about a minute, a slow-motion attempt on Cass's part to scratch out his eyes, while Gard held her hands and laughed. She knew he was laughing because of the air bubbles coming out of his mouth.

Bursting from the surface, Cass gasped for oxygen. Gard came up right behind her, also sucking in air in big gulps. "Obviously you intend keeping me in here," Cass said while coughing and gasping.

"Obviously."

"Why?" If looks could kill, Gard would have fallen over dead from the one Cass laid on him.

He began untying the shirt from around his waist. "Seems like a good place to talk."

"You threw me in this damned pool to talk? Have you lost your mind?"

"Don't think so. On second thought... maybe a little."

"Maybe a lot," she snapped. Her eyes narrowed in speculation when he lifted his right foot so he could pull off his boot and sock, but then it hit her. He was undressing!

Well, *she* wasn't undressing, not if he held her in this pool for three days!

There were different levels to the pool's configuration. Wearing as frigid an expression as she could muster, Cass sat on a rock so that only her head and shoulders were above the waterline. She didn't turn her eyes or pretend maidenly embarrassment. If he was crude enough to undress in front of her again, she was crude enough to watch and angry enough to pray that her steady, disdainful gaze would embarrass *him*.

It didn't work. He finished taking off his clothes without even a hint of embarrassment. Cass stewed during the process, but when he was completely nude and looking at her, she began to worry.

"Aren't you uncomfortable in all those clothes?" he asked softly.

"No, and don't you come near me!"

He grinned. "Fine. I'll sit here and you sit over there."

She didn't believe him, not for a second, especially when he began moving around the pool. "Just looking for a rock to sit on," he said casually. "Oh, there's one."

It was much too close to her rock. "Find one farther away from me," she said sharply.

"Aren't any."

"There are so! Damn you, Gard, you're not going to talk me into anything."

With his eyes crinkling in amusement, he sat down. "Of course I'm not. Just want to talk about things in general."

"You're a damned liar," she mumbled, turning her face so she wouldn't have to look at him. The water was much too clear, and every manly asset he possessed was right there in plain sight.

Leaning back, Gard put his elbows on the rock ledge of the pool. "Now, let me see. What were we talking about? Oh, yes, I remember. The fact that you made love with me when you didn't like me. Appears as though you did that twice, but correct me if I'm wrong. Maybe you liked me the second time. I guess that's possible."

She shot him a dirty look. "Think again."

"Now, that's really puzzling. Do you usually make love with men you don't like?" Gard quickly held up a hand. "Mind you, I'm not judging. If that's what you do, then that's what you do. But you know, I got to thinking about that today while I was hiking around, and you just don't strike me as a woman who takes her pleasure wherever she finds it. I'm pretty sure you can see why I'm puzzled."

He received another dirty look. "Drop dead, Sterling."

"You know what I think? I think you'd rather kiss me than fight with me. I think you like me when you'd rather hate me, and I think you felt the same way fourteen years ago."

Eleven

Shocked at his perception, Cass twisted around and tried to climb out of the pool. Gard was on her in a heartbeat, pulling her back into the water. She splashed and squirmed and tried to escape, but he was too much for her.

"Admit I'm right," he challenged, holding her wrists and looking into her eyes. "If you can be that honest."

Her only chance to get out of this unscathed was a strong offense, she decided, lifting her chin defiantly. "After all the conniving and scheming you've done, you have the nerve to mention honesty? Was it your innate honesty that blackmailed me into coming out here? I can't believe you would accuse me of dishonesty when *you're* behaving like a . . . a savage!"

Gard couldn't help laughing, though it was obvious that Cass was only using anger to evade giving him an answer. "A savage, did you say?"

"You heard what I said. And I meant it, too. Throwing me into this pool and then forcing me to stay here. If that's civilized behavior in your crowd, I hope I never have the misfortune of meeting your friends." She gave her wrists a jerk, trying to break his hold on them and failing.

Gard barely noticed. "The only reason you're angry is because I figured you out."

She scoffed. "I've figured you out, too, Gard Sterling, and your lurid imagination is surpassed only by your astronomical ego. Now, let go of me and let me get out of this pool, or so help me, I will never speak to you again for as long as I live."

Gard's smile faded. He'd been so sure. Could his theory be that far off base?

"Okay, supposing I'm wrong," he said slowly. "But if I am, if you never thought two hoots about me years ago, how come you made love with me at the sand dunes?"

"Oh, for crying out loud," Cass snapped. "Doesn't everyone have at least one escapade in their life they wish had never happened? Count that night as mine, okay?"

Gard studied her face, her eyes. Was she lying? What she'd said wasn't exactly flattering, but considering his reputation at the time, it had a ring of truth. He wasn't completely satisfied, however.

"What about the second time?" he asked flatly.

Cass sucked in a startled breath. "Uh, another mistake."

"Apparently you keep making sexual mistakes with men you don't like."

"I most certainly do not! You're the only..." She stopped, because the expression in his eyes had become much too knowing.

"I'm the only man you've made those kinds of mistakes with. Was that what you were going to say?"

"Do you give a damn that I'm getting waterlogged?" she yelled.

"Answer my question, Cass!" She was the most evasive person he'd ever known, and his good humor was really starting to taper off.

"Don't you dare shout at me," she said threateningly.

"It's all right for you to yell, but it's not okay for me? Cass, you're driving me crazy."

"*I'm* driving *you* crazy? What do you think you're doing to me?"

She was going to say more, a *lot* more, but she was suddenly yanked forward and into his arms. His lips came down on hers hard and possessively, as though he had every right to kiss her. To prove that he didn't, Cass dug her fingernails into his bare chest.

He jerked his head up, then looked down at the scratches on his chest with a puzzled expression. "Why'd you do that?"

"I could ask you the same question." Glaring at him, Cass realized that he was no longer hanging on to her. Quickly she lunged for the edge of the pool and climbed out.

This time Gard didn't stop her. Scowling, he stood in the pool and watched her running to her tent, dripping water with every hasty step. Perplexed, he sat on the same rock Cass had used. Maybe she *didn't* want wild and reckless.

But, dammit to hell, his questions were valid. If she hadn't liked him way back when, why had she made love with him? And if she still didn't like him after all those years, why had she cooperated at the dunes and done it again?

Something didn't add up. Gard's eyes narrowed. He *had* figured Cass out, only she wouldn't admit it. In fact, his knowing the truth and saying so had turned her upside down.

Maybe this camping idea wasn't a good idea, he thought with the ache of disappointment in his gut. If all they were going to do was bicker, what was the point? He had honestly expected her to relax and enjoy being out here. This was such a beautiful place, how could anyone not enjoy it?

In her tent, Cass got out of her wet clothes. She wasn't a bit cold, but she was trembling as if chilled to the bone. It was an inner eruption, she realized, caused by Gard's surprising insight. He must have been doing some serious thinking to grasp the feelings she had experienced fourteen years ago.

Well, it wasn't something she was going to discuss with him, no matter how hard he pushed. Dressing quickly, she took a peek outside, saw that Gard was still in the hot pool, then hurriedly carried her drenched things to the line he had strung between two trees for drying towels and such. The second her shorts, T-shirt and underwear were draped over the line, she scurried back into her tent.

Gard had watched her from the pool, and he thought again that maybe this camping trip had been a mistake. Being alone together for a week had struck him as the perfect way to get through to Cass. Apparently not. Or, at least, it sure wasn't working yet. Should he give up and break camp? Cass would probably jump at the chance to leave.

He rubbed his mouth thoughtfully. Was he ready to give up on Cass? Maybe he should wait another day to see what happened.

Yes, that was what he would do... give it one more day. If nothing changed, he would break camp tomorrow and tell Cass why, in the bargain. If she was going to remain determined to keep them apart, there really wasn't much he could do about it. He sure didn't like the idea of defeat, but there it was, staring him in the face.

Pulling himself out of the pool, he gathered his clothes and headed for his own tent.

Cass was towel-drying her hair again, this time within the relative safety of her tent. Sounds from outside made her stop and listen. Then she realized what she was hearing: Gard was doing the breakfast dishes.

Fine, she thought peevishly. Let him do them. He really didn't deserve any consideration from her. Let him do *all* the work. With the way he'd behaved since their ridiculous meeting at the Plantation, she shouldn't even be speaking to him.

Her hair was reasonably dry and tied back with a length of yarn when she heard Gard just outside her tent.

"Cass?"

"What?"

"I'm going fishing. Would you like to come along?"

"No, thank you," she said icily.

"Kind of figured you'd say that," he replied grimly. "I'll be gone a couple of hours. About like yesterday."

"So go," she mumbled under her breath, glad to be rid of him. The tent was heating up from the sun and she would like to be outside. "Fine," she said out loud.

"See you later."

"Okay."

When he walked off, she sighed with relief. Moving the flap a mere fraction, she peeked out and saw that he was picking up his tackle box and fishing pole. In the next minute he left camp and she breathed another relieved sigh.

Heaving the flap wide open, she secured it with its heavy-duty snaps, then did the same with the window. A lovely little breeze immediately floated through the tent, cooling her feverish skin.

The shakes had passed, thank goodness, though she certainly couldn't deny that her emotions were still in an uproar. He knew too much about her now. She could deny ever having any affection for him until doomsday and he wouldn't believe her. He was a much more logical thinker than she'd given him credit for, and it only made sense that she must have felt something for him to make love with him.

"Damn," Cass muttered. Did she want Gard? And if she did, in what capacity? What was in *his* mind, an affair or something more?

The truth, which was something she *couldn't* deny, was that she did want Gard. Sexually, that is. But how could she give in to desire and pretend that nothing else mattered when he'd been putting her through the wringer on that contract?

Now she was even ambiguous on that matter. Maybe she didn't want to sell the ranch, after all. Maybe she wasn't so positive about buying into the Deering Gallery, even if she did sell.

Everything was up in the air, every single aspect of her life. She wasn't painting, her goals had all gone to hell in a hand basket, and there was no one to blame but Gard.

She wasn't painting. The phrase stuck in her mind, and she eyed the black canvas bag containing her supplies. Determination to produce something seemed suddenly crucial, and she grabbed the large bag and carried it outside. Looking around, she decided to set up near the lake, and she lugged the bag to the shore.

Kneeling, she unzipped it and took out her easel, which had been disassembled to fit into the bag. It took about five minutes to put it, together whereupon she glanced at the sun, then placed the easel in what she figured was the best light.

She laid out paints and palettes, set a new canvas on the easel, took a deep breath and began.

Gard returned around four, which was hours longer than he'd told Cass he would be gone. But the solitude had been healing and he had lingered until an unfamiliar idea struck him: he wanted Cass as his wife. The thought had come like a bolt of lightning, almost scaring him. Not that the idea of marriage itself was frightening, but Cass's attitude sure was. If he proposed to her in her present frame of mind, she was apt to sock him. He knew she felt something for him, she would never be able to convince him otherwise. But she was keeping her emotions so tightly held, was it possible for him to break through her guard?

Sad to say, he'd done nothing right since their meeting at the Plantation. Hell, he hadn't done anything right with Cass since they were kids. Small wonder she didn't trust him.

He entered camp and set down his fishing gear near his tent. Spotting Cass sitting on the ground down by the lake, he wished he had the nerve to walk up to her and announce his feelings with neither hesitation nor fanfare. How would she react to a sudden declaration of undying love?

Drawing an uneasy breath, Gard slowly started walking in Cass's direction. He was almost there when he noticed the easel and canvas, and the canvas bag he'd wondered about lying open on the grass.

Cass looked up. "Oh, you're back." She'd been so deep in thought that she hadn't heard him until he was only a few feet away.

Her calm voice and expression surprised Gard. Pleased him, too. "Hi. You've been painting. Mind if I take a look?"

"Um..." Her painting made her nervous. It was even more dramatic than her first successful abstract, and she was almost afraid to let herself like it.

But she couldn't hide her work in a closet. People had to see it if she wanted to remain a viable artist.

"Sure, go ahead," she said in a rather thin voice.

Gard walked around both her and the easel. The painting wasn't at all what he'd expected. From the one painting of Cass's that he'd seen hanging over the fireplace in the Whitfield living room, he had anticipated a pretty, softly hued picture of the countryside. Instead there were unusual colors, textures and designs on the canvas, and it was as though the combination and result reached out and punched him in the gut.

He blinked, narrowed his eyes and looked at it again. Cass swallowed nervously, waiting to hear what he thought of it. Not that his opinion would count for much. By his own admission, he wasn't into art. And even those people who were didn't always like abstracts.

"Is the earth really moving or am I feeling an earthquake from this painting?" Gard asked.

"What?" Cass's eyes widened in genuine surprise.

"This is really something," he mumbled, almost to himself. He didn't understand the painting, but there was no ignoring its impact. He finally tore his eyes from the canvas and looked at Cass. "I didn't know you did things like this."

Startled, Cass got to her feet. "Do you like it?"

"I don't know how to answer that. It... does something to me. I've never seen anything like it."

Excitement began sparking in Cass's eyes. "*What* does it do to you?"

"I don't know if I can explain it." His gaze was on the painting again. "I feel... sort of jagged." He gave a short laugh at his inept explanation. "It's not a soothing painting, is it?"

"No, it's not. Do you understand abstract expressionism?"

He laughed sharply again. "I've never even heard of it."

"It's more emotion than substance. What I mean is, I wasn't attempting to paint a mountain or anything specific. It's self-expressive."

"Meaning, it came from inside you?"

"Something like that."

Gard turned to face her. "This is the way you feel inside?"

"I... suppose so." Thinking about it for a moment, she added, "It's not how I feel now. It's as though I transferred my feelings to the canvas."

He could see that she was much calmer than before he'd gone fishing. He tried to relate what Cass had done to alleviate her tension to his own life. When problems stacked up, didn't he take a long horseback ride and return to the ranch feeling better equipped to cope?

But riding for a few hours and creating a stunning work of art weren't the same thing at all. His gaze flicked back to the painting. "I really didn't know how talented you are," he said quietly. "Your work must be very important to you."

"Well... yes... it is." She was almost embarrassed by Gard's praise, which she certainly hadn't expected. A need to explain herself arose. "This type of work is new to me.

I've really only done one other abstract that I consider good. A gallery in San Francisco has been showing and selling my paintings." She laughed a little nervously. "Francis, the owner of the gallery, doesn't even know I've been dabbling in this style."

"I'd hardly call this piece 'dabbling,'" Gard returned, speaking in a serious vein. "You know I'm no expert on any kind of art, Cass, but for what it's worth, I think you've produced an incredible painting here."

A thrill rocketed through her. Even though he had no experience whatsoever with art, Gard's favorable opinion lifted her spirits as no one else's ever had.

"That's very nice of you to say," she murmured, her gaze on the painting. Was it really good? Certainly it was dramatic and emotional. If she was going to continue this style of work, she really had to obtain an expert's opinion of it. She was, after all, earning her living from her paintings, and if her abstracts weren't salable, she should return to her former style.

She frowned slightly at a new thought: she didn't ever have to pick up another paintbrush if she didn't want to. As sole owner of the Whitfield Land and Cattle Company, she could operate the ranch and never have to worry about income again. Then there was her other option, which was at the heart of the present upheaval in her life: selling out. If she sold and didn't use the money to buy that interest in the gallery from Francis, she could live on the proceeds for the rest of her days. Everything really hinged on where she wanted to live, Oregon, Montana, or California.

But never paint again? No, that was an impossible idea. Even so, she didn't need any expert opinions to keep going. For the first time, really, Cass realized that she had the means—sadly obtained from her father's estate—to paint in any style she wished, salable or not.

Those thoughts raced through her mind so quickly, Gard was still studying the painting when she shook herself back to the present and her surroundings. The intensity of his interest astounded Cass. It was as though he had forgotten she was there, as though he was off in another world.

She cleared her throat. "There's a breeze coming up. I'd better take the canvas into my tent so dust doesn't get blown into the wet paint."

Gard turned his head to look at her. There was the strangest expression on his face, one that Cass couldn't decipher. Then he took note of the breeze and glanced up at the sky. "There are a few clouds rolling in. We could have some rain tonight."

Cass started for the painting. Gard put a hand on her arm, stopping her. "I'll carry it in for you," he said. The professionalism of Cass's work shook him. He didn't have to understand art to recognize talent when he saw it. For some reason, he had never given any consideration to her career. He'd been thinking in terms of the two of them, living in Montana, of course, picturing them as a ranching couple. He felt let down, because a woman with her abilities wasn't apt to exchange a career such as hers for anything, especially for a man who'd been little more than a thorn in her side.

Not that he would ever, under any circumstances, ask her to give up painting, but there had to be a reason why she lived in Oregon rather than Montana and it only seemed sensible to think that it was because of her career.

Cautiously lifting the canvas from the easel and carrying it toward her tent, he tried to sort through his confused thoughts. This painting proved Cass could produce in Montana. Location probably didn't influence her work at all, so why *was* she living in Oregon?

Cass trudged behind him, carrying the easel. She, too, was battling confusion. There were too many loose ends in her life right now.

"Gard, let me go in first," she said as they got near her tent.

He nodded. "Right."

Cass slipped around him and entered the tent. Setting the easel in a corner opposite to her bed, she stepped back so Gard could place the painting on the stand. Then he stepped back and looked at it again.

"It looks different in this light, doesn't it?" he said.

"Any change of lighting will affect it."

Gard shook his head slightly, as though he couldn't quite believe what he was seeing. "It's beautiful, Cass."

"Beautiful?" Blinking in surprise, she moved closer to Gard and tried to see the painting through his eyes. She cocked her head to one side. "I don't think I would call it beautiful, but it does have a certain impact, doesn't it?"

"Definitely." Gard felt her next to him. He also felt the predictable reaction in his groin from her nearness. He wanted to groan out loud. Why were they at such odds? Why couldn't they communicate like an ordinary couple?

Then again, maybe neither of them had ever been ordinary. Cass certainly wasn't, not when she could turn out a painting like this one in an afternoon. As for him, he'd been considering himself pretty damned ordinary the past few years. But Cass's memories of Gard Sterling were mostly from many years ago, and he sure hadn't been run-of-the-mill in those days.

The tent suddenly seemed like a private little nook to him. He glanced to the bed, dampened his lips and turned slightly to look at Cass. Her head came around. "What?" Then she saw the expression in his eyes and her heart began fluttering.

Nervously she started backing toward the tent opening. "I have to get the rest of my things." She had already cleaned her brushes before Gard's return, so it was merely a matter of closing up the canvas case and bringing it inside.

"Please don't run away," he said softly, taking a forward step for each one she took away from him. "Cass, I've been a damned fool with you, but I swear that's over. We've got to have a meeting of the minds. There must be a way."

Before she reached the opening, his hands rose to clasp her upper arms. The intensity of his blue eyes took Cass's breath. "I really, uh, we shouldn't... you can't..." Her stammering made no sense whatsoever, especially when she was standing still and drowning in the depths of his eyes.

"Cass, there are things I'd like to say to you."

"No," she whispered. "I don't want to hear them."

"You know what they are, don't you?"

She gave her head one small shake. "No... and I don't want to know."

His gaze roamed her face, lingering at each lovely feature. What lay behind her beautiful green eyes? Why wouldn't she let him speak?

Well, there were other ways of communicating. He pulled her forward, toward him. Not quickly or roughly, but with definite purpose. He saw the pupils of her eyes enlarge and heard her sharp intake of air.

Cass wondered if she hadn't poured all of her abrasive emotions into her painting, as all she felt now was the softness of desire. She'd been thinking too often of the way he had made love to her on the trunk of her car, and the memory was upon her again, strong and influencing.

"Cass..." he whispered before settling his lips on hers.

She shivered at the contact and then snuggled against his body, as though needing his warmth. His mouth played with hers, teasing it open, wetting it with his tongue.

You're a fool, flashed through her mind, but she didn't have the willpower to push him away. Instead she took his kiss and gave her own, at the same time wrapping her arms around his waist.

Gard truly hadn't expected her to respond. Certainly he didn't understand it. Dazed and dizzy, he buried the questions and concentrated on the pleasure of holding her. Of kissing her. Of touching her.

His hands began wandering, caressing her from shoulders to hips. Her participation was earthshaking. While he yanked the bottom of her blouse from her shorts, she did the same with his shirt. She wasn't going to stop him, he realized while trying to catch his breath between kisses. Incredible.

More confident, he undid the buttons on her blouse and pushed it off her shoulders. Then, so it seemed, neither of them could get undressed fast enough. They fell to Cass's bed, with her on her back and Gard on top of her. Kisses were exchanged greedily, hungrily.

"I want you so much," he whispered raggedly.

He hadn't had to say it, not when she was already lying under him. But the words lifted her to a higher plane of desire and she opened her legs for him. He put the two of them together as one did a jigsaw puzzle, with all of the curves and angles fitting to form a perfect picture.

Then he began moving, raising his head to watch her face while he loved her. He wanted to say it. *I love you, Cass.* But she wasn't yet ready to hear it. She would make love with him, but she wouldn't talk about love.

She would, he decided grimly. Before they slept tonight.

Of course, tonight was still several hours away, and how could a man be discontented when he was deep in the throes of a blinding passion with the woman he hoped to make his life partner?

No, he wasn't a bit discontented. The way the blood was rushing around in his head, it was a wonder he could think at all.

He quit trying and put every ounce of energy into giving both Cass and himself pleasure.

Twelve

The light was waning in the tent. Cass was lying on her right side, facing the painting, peering at it in the dim light and wondering if it was really good and if maybe now that she had two abstracts she shouldn't at least talk to Francis about them. Gard, too, was on his right side, with his left arm across Cass's waist and his left leg thrown over hers. Unlike her, his eyes were closed.

Neither had said much after their tumultuous lovemaking. Gard kept expecting Cass to ask him to leave, and instead she seemed quite content to lie in his arms. He appeared calm, also, although it was all show. Inside he was a mass of nerves. Was this the right time to talk about love and marriage? Would there ever be a "right" time? How did a man know? One thing he did know was that they had to talk.

He opened his eyes. "Cass?"

"Hmm?"

"Everything all right?"

It took a moment for her to answer. "Not exactly."

He raised up to his elbow to peer down at her, which told him little as he could only see her profile. "Meaning?" he asked.

She drew in a long, slow breath. "Don't you feel a little silly about blackmailing me into coming out here?"

Hesitating, he finally nodded. "Yeah, guess I do. Cass, I can give you my answer on that option right now, if you want to hear it."

She turned onto her back to see his face. "You could have given me an answer weeks ago, couldn't you?"

"Yes."

"Why didn't you?"

"I don't know. After meeting you again I started thinking weird thoughts. Like...could I keep you in Montana by delaying my answer? And why was I just now noticing how unique and beautiful you were when we'd been neighbors most of our lives?"

She probed the depths of his eyes. "No lines, okay? I have a lot on my mind, and I really can't cope with macho lines right now."

"I have a lot on my mind, too, Cass," he said softly. "Have you ever been in love?"

She stared. "Where on earth did that come from?"

"It's something I'd like to know."

"Have you?" she returned.

He smiled. "I asked you first."

She turned back onto her side. "Obviously neither of us wants to talk about it, if we were."

Slowly he lowered his head to the pillow. "Do you want to hear my answer on that option now?"

"You know something, Gard? I really don't care one way or the other what you've decided. It could be completely irrelevant now because I've been thinking about keeping the ranch. It's not certain yet, but... I've been thinking about it."

His pulse began speeding. "Then you'd be staying in Montana?"

"That's one of the questions I've been struggling with. The reason I wanted to sell in the first place was to buy into the San Francisco gallery that's been handling my paintings. Now I'm not sure." She heaved a sigh. "I'm not sure of anything anymore."

He spoke quietly. "Do you consider making love with me again as another mistake?"

She laughed mirthlessly. "I don't know what to call it. Obviously you affect me sexually." Her shoulder lifted in a small shrug. "As I said, I've got a lot on my mind. A lot to think about," she added after a moment. "I wish the answers would come out of the blue and I would suddenly understand myself and...and what I want."

"You're saying you don't know what you want? In connection with your career, or what?"

"With everything, career included."

"I'm in there someplace, aren't I? Mixed in with all your other questions?"

She sighed again, softly this time. "Why deny it? Yes, you're a part of my quandary. I never wanted to...well, you know."

"Never wanted to like me," he said in a husky whisper. "I've upset your equilibrium, haven't I?"

"To say the least. What's almost impossible to believe is that I'm accepting your intrusion in my life. My confusion is all your fault, and I'm accepting it." Another sigh whispered through her lips.

"Not always," Gard murmured.

"No, not always. Sometimes I'm strong enough to say no, and then something like this happens and I realize that I'm not always strong. Or sensible."

"But only where I'm concerned. Cass, doesn't that tell you something?"

"It sure does," she said with a cynical little laugh. "It tells me I should stay the hell away from you. Which is one of the reasons I'm so torn about the ranch. If I did keep it, and live there, would you leave me alone?"

"Not on a bet," he said softly. He took his hand from around her waist and ran it down her side, clear to her knees. "I love touching you."

A shiver of pleasure danced along her skin. She couldn't help responding to his touch, sensible or not. "So," she said a bit breathlessly, "you started thinking about keeping me in Montana at our meeting at the Plantation."

"For me it was as though we were meeting for the first time. I wanted to know you better, which couldn't happen with you in Oregon." He'd spoken a little cautiously, unsure of how long Cass's good mood was going to last. Considering how *she* must have felt at that meeting, his confession could significantly alter her mood. He went one daring step further. "I barely remembered you, and when you walked into that room..."

"I get the idea," Cass broke in coolly. "That's probably a subject we shouldn't get into."

"The past, you mean. Cass, we really should talk about it."

She stiffened slightly. "I don't think so." Connecting the past with their present relationship—whatever it was—was extremely discomfiting. It was much easier for her to think of Gard as a new acquaintance than as the rebellious young man she had all but worshiped at seventeen. And it still hurt that he didn't remember the most romantic night of her life.

She winced. Their first time at the dunes was *still* the most romantic night of her life? Wasn't that a rather sad commentary on her love life in general?

Of course, she had dedicated herself to her art, and the few men she had allowed to get beyond her front door had been more friends than lovers. In truth, Gard had hurt her so badly she had never really trusted men very much.

Now, here she was, lying in his arms. In the arms of the man who had ruined her for any other man. It was stupid. Why couldn't she control her damned libido with Gard?

Gard heard her rather forlorn sigh. "What's wrong, honey?"

She gave a brief, rather brittle laugh. "Us...like this." She sat up suddenly. "Gard, I want to go home."

The mood swing he'd been expecting had happened. Frowning, he sat up. "Cassie, listen to me for a minute, okay? We've got something special going for us. We could have it all, honey, but we need more time together. This place is perfect. We're alone and..."

"No," she said firmly. Then she heard the rain on the tent, starting abruptly and coming down hard.

Gard heard it, too. "Cass, I can't break camp in the rain."

She turned to glare at him. "A little rain won't kill you."

"No, but everything's under cover right now, and I don't want my camping gear to get soaked. It would take a lot of time and work to get it dried out later on."

It was a pretty lame excuse for staying, Cass thought irately. But it was his stuff, and if he didn't want it to get wet...well, maybe he wasn't wrong. It seemed as though even the weather was plotting to keep her here.

Gard clasped his hand around her shoulder. "Come on. Lie down again. Listen to the rain."

She thought of telling him to go and listen to the rain in his own tent, but the words got stuck in her throat. Her weakness for Gard was not a plus, in her estimation, but it wasn't something she could eradicate just because she wished it.

He urged her down with a little tug on her shoulder. "Come on, honey. You'll get chilled sitting there with nothing on."

"I *could* get dressed," she observed.

"Please don't."

The soft, sensual tone of his voice raised goose bumps on Cass's skin. Or maybe she was already getting chilled. Whatever, she knew his body was warm and sleek, and that he would offer her every physical comfort known to mankind.

Gard began tugging the sleeping bag this way and that, opening it so they could crawl into it. The rain was definitely lowering the temperature and he, himself, was feeling the chill. He wriggled his way into the bag.

He smiled, though Cass was looking the other way and didn't see it. "Come on, honey. Snuggle with me."

Sighing, she gave up and crawled in. He zipped the bag around them, then burrowed an arm beneath her head and cradled it on his shoulder.

"Perfect," he murmured huskily, stroking the silky skin of her abdomen with his free hand.

Was there anything more intimate than two people zipped into a sleeping bag? Cass thought with a strange mixture of panic and pleasure.

The panic died through logic. What was the point of panicking now? Hadn't she already proved—several times—what a fool she was for Gard? Proving it again wouldn't make a dram of difference in the history of the world.

Besides, the pleasure was unbelievable. It was an oversize sleeping bag, thank goodness, as Gard was a big man and taking up a lot of space. But there was no way to lie with him and not feel every inch of his hot and sexy body touching some portion of hers.

He was nuzzling her ear. "I could do this every day of my life with you, sweetheart," he whispered.

So could she, she realized, biting her lip and frowning slightly. But then his hand slipped lower on her belly and she stopped frowning. He moved her leg on top of his, opening her for his hand.

"Gard," she whispered, all set to protest his boldness.

"Yes?" Gently he began exploring her most secret spot.

Her eyes closed. "Uh, nothing."

He chuckled softly in her ear. "Tell me you like what I'm doing."

What he was doing was making her blood pressure soar. "I think you can tell I like it," she said, her voice hoarse and thick. She managed a challenging, gravelly laugh. "Let's see if *you* like it."

Her hand slowly glided downward from his waist, whereupon she encircled his hard and erect manhood.

"Ohhh," he groaned. "Yeah, I like it. I like it a lot." Crooking his elbow under her head, he brought her face around and took her mouth in a long and drugging kiss.

When they both needed air, he broke the kiss. Cass gasped out, "Oh, I'm so hot."

"Me, too, babe."

"I mean, *I'm hot!* Unzip this bag and let me cool off."

"I don't want you to cool off. I *want* you hot."

"Gard, I'm sweating."

"Yeah, that's the whole idea." He moved on top of her and slid into her velvety heat. "See, there's something special about making love in a sleeping bag."

"Apparently you've done it before."

"Nope. Just heard about it."

"Liar." But the word was said like a caress. He was moving very slowly inside her, driving her wild. She planted her hands on his buttocks and closed her eyes.

The explosion within her took her by storm. Tears spilled from her eyes, and she buried her face in Gard's throat until the spasms had passed.

He tipped her chin and made her look at him. "That was only the beginning."

She had no idea what he was talking about. Naturally he would need to reach fulfillment, as she had, but for some reason he seemed to be referring to her.

He hugged her and kissed the tears from her face. Then he began kissing her mouth, little feathery kisses that were pleasant and soothing. In the back of her mind, however, Cass wondered why he wasn't rushing to his own completion.

His mouth began lingering on hers, and one of his hands tenderly fondled her breasts. She was surprised to feel a darting pleasure when he toyed with her nipples. After all, it was no more than an hour ago that she had been wonderfully satisfied, and just now, again. Surely she couldn't respond so quickly to more lovemaking, could she?

She had her answer when his hips began moving, again very slowly, and the thrills of release were again upon her. "Oh, Gard," she cried.

"That's it," he whispered. "That's what I wanted."

Breathing hard, she stared into his eyes with a stunned expression. "I—I've never..."

"Good, I'm glad." He kissed and petted her for a few minutes, lying quite still upon her, then began moving again.

It happened repeatedly, over and over, that incredible tempest and feverish pleasure. She couldn't believe that she was capable of this kind of lovemaking. She'd read about it, of course, but never had she experienced anything even close to what Gard was doing to her.

She became physically weaker with each climax, and finally she could take no more. "Gard...please." It was barely a croak.

"All right, sweetheart. One last ride." This time it wasn't slow and easy, but rough and hard and fast. To Cass's amazement, she cried out when he did.

Utterly drained, she lay there with her eyes closed and feeling as though she would never be able to move again. Gard moved to lie beside her, his arms around her, and neither said a word for a very long time.

Cass finally opened her eyes. "It's dark." The rain on the tent was lulling, and she shut her eyes again and fell asleep.

While Cass slept, Gard stared into the dark and thought. What would come next? When she woke up, would she be receptive to hearing his feelings? He'd sworn to tell her before tonight, but tonight was upon them and he hadn't said a word.

Hunger suddenly seized him. He hadn't eaten since breakfast and his stomach was growling in protest.

But could he get out of the sleeping bag without disturbing Cass? He grinned in the dark, pleased that he'd worn her out in the most pleasurable way possible. She had to love him. Women didn't respond to men they didn't love the way Cass responded to him. Getting her to admit it, to face it, though, wasn't going to be easy. But nothing had been easy with Cass, so what else was new?

His stomach growled again; he had to get something to eat. Slowly and carefully, he slid upward in the sleeping bag, sitting up gradually. Cass never budged, not even when he left the bed completely and felt around in the dark for his clothes and got dressed. It was pouring rain, so he stealthily found his socks and boots and pulled them on.

Slipping outside, he made a dash for the canvas he'd strung to protect their kitchen and eating area. Everything—the food boxes, eating utensils, stove and tiny refrigerator—was under the canvas roof and only a little damp. Before getting some food, though, he ran to his tent for a jacket. The temperature had dropped a good thirty degrees, and his shirt just wasn't heavy enough for him to stay warm.

Then he ate, wolfing down a thick sandwich of cold meat, cheese, lettuce, tomatoes and dill pickles. Sitting at the table then, he watched the rain and thought about Cass. She would probably want to go home in the morning, which was unfortunate when they were finally making some real headway.

Thoughtfully he eyed his truck. An idea came to him and he smiled.

Fifteen minutes later he returned to Cass's tent. As silently and cautiously as he had stolen away, he undressed and slid back into the sleeping bag with her. She stirred slightly, but stayed asleep.

It was a good omen, he felt, settling himself down and closing his eyes.

He was asleep in minutes.

* * *

Cass awoke in a sweat. Groggily she realized it was morning, the rain had stopped and the tent felt like a sauna. Slithering out of the sleeping bag, she looked at Gard sleeping peacefully and recalled last night. It was a stunning recollection, because last night had been one for the books.

Unnerved, she put on her robe, grabbed some towels and her toothbrush, stuck her feet into a pair of thongs and left the tent. Outside she located Gard's special soap and shampoo, then made her way to the lake.

The sun was bright in a clear sky; the storm had passed. Tossing the robe, she waded into the water, lowered herself until the water reached her chin and sighed with intense pleasure. First she brushed her teeth. Then she took a swim, enjoying the exercise, and finally she bathed and shampooed her hair.

Last night troubled her, but she kept pushing thoughts of it to the back of her mind. She knew that eventually she was going to have to deal with it, but she wasn't up to doing so at the moment. Later, she thought, though "later" probably wouldn't be any easier. Especially after Gard showed his face.

"Damn," she whispered, sinking into the water until only her nose and eyes were showing. Gard would expect something from last night. She had to prepare herself for whatever it was.

The rain had cooled the lake water considerably. Feeling a little chilled, Cass got out, picked up her towels and wandered over to the hot pools. Choosing the one Gard had thrown her in yesterday, she stepped into the deliciously hot water and sat on her rock.

Okay, she commanded herself, think! Of course, it was only sensible to demand that Gard take her home. That went without saying. But what if he refused? What if he had plans for the rest of the week, plans that included sleeping together at night, and probably a lot of fooling around during the day?

Her heart skipped a beat. A few days of sin and sex wouldn't be that terrible, would they? After all, she'd already done the worst.

Actually, wasn't Gard a much lesser concern than her decision with the ranch? And how about the gallery? You also have a house in Oregon to worry about, she told herself. And your work? Are you going to call Francis and tell her about the abstracts, or are you going to return to your former style of painting?

"Good morning!"

Cass turned her head to see Gard heading for the pool, stark naked and carrying a towel. She smiled weakly. "Good morning."

"Is this a great day, or what?" he said with a big smile while sliding into the pool. He waded over to her, took her chin and kissed her on the mouth. His eyes contained warmth, caring and tenderness, Cass saw, and wondered if he was putting on an act for her benefit. "How're you doing this morning?"

"Um, fine. I'm fine." Memories of last night embarrassed her, burning her cheeks pink, and she averted her eyes to avoid his.

Gard caught on and decided this game had gone on long enough. "There's something I have to tell you, Cass."

He was still leaning over her, his face mere inches from hers. "Oh?" she said, immediately wary. "If it's about the contract, I told you..."

"It's not. It's about us, you and me."

She sucked in a suddenly nervous breath. "I—I don't think I want to hear it."

"Tough tamales, sweetheart. You're going to hear it, like it or not. I happen to be in love with you. Seriously in love. The marrying kind of love." Cass was staring at him as though he'd just sprouted horns. "Don't look at me that way. Tell me you love me, too."

She went limp and lay back against the rock ledge of the pool.

"Cass?"

"What?" she whispered.

"Don't you have *something* to say?"

She'd known he would expect something from her because of last night. But love? Marriage?

"Right at the moment, no," she said in a reedy, thin voice.

"Nothing at all?" Worry lines creased Gard's forehead. "Maybe I shouldn't have sprung it on you like that. I probably picked a bad time."

She had to say something, she realized. A yes, a no, or a go to hell, but something.

"Uh, when did this, uh, when did you..."

"You're stammering, honey. I really shook you, didn't I?"

She nodded, her first vigorous movement since he'd gotten into the pool. "Gard, I never dreamed..."

Now that hurt. His lips thinned, and he moved away from her to occupy another rock. "It never occurred to you that I was falling in love?"

"You've hardly behaved as if you were. I mean, those nasty letters from your attorney and...all." Her voice trailed off.

"Foreplay."

"Foreplay?" she repeated numbly. He loved her. My God, he wanted to marry her! Her head was spinning like a top.

He forced a laugh. "You just need a little time to get used to the idea, Cass."

She was starting to recover. "I don't think that's it."

His smile vanished. "So, what is?"

She blinked at him. "I—I don't know." If he had proposed to her when she was seventeen she would have probably fainted from happiness. If he had merely had the courtesy to recognize her on the street after taking her virginity, she would have been giddy with joy. Those old hurts were still with her, she realized again, still causing her pain.

And he knew none of it. Other than that they had made love at the sand dunes one summer night.

She heaved herself up and out of the water, reaching for her towels to immediately cover herself. "I want you to take me home. Please break camp so we can leave."

"Right now?"

"Yes, right now."

"Cass, we haven't even had breakfast. Can't you wait for an hour or so?"

"I'm not hungry. I want to go home."

Was she on the verge of tears? "All right, fine," Gard agreed wearily. "I'll break camp. We'll leave as soon as I'm finished."

"Thank you." Walking away, the tears she had been holding back only through supreme effort finally escaped. By the time she had gathered her robe from the shore of the lake and went into her tent, she was sobbing uncontrollably.

Throwing herself onto the tangle of sheets and sleeping bag, she clenched her fists and pounded the bedding. "Damn you," she moaned. "How dare you suggest love and marriage to me now? How dare you?"

Thirteen

Last night's clothes were in Cass's tent, but Gard went to his own for fresh things. Dressed and stocking-footed—he'd brought only one pair of boots—he left his tent and walked to Cass's. Hesitating only a moment, he pushed the flap aside and stepped in. She was dressed in jeans and a blouse, but she was on the bed, huddled and crying.

"What are you afraid of?" His voice sounded loud, even to his ears.

"What?" Sitting up, she quickly dashed the tears from beneath her eyes. "I didn't hear you come in. You should have said something before barging in. You have no right—"

He held up a hand. "Stop right there."

She had never seen his face look so hard and unyielding. "I don't want you in here. Please leave."

"No. We're going to have a little talk, and I'm going to start the discussion by apologizing for not remembering our night together fourteen years ago." He sank to sit cross-legged on the floor without once taking his eyes off of her. "You hated me for that, didn't you? For not remembering?"

She attempted a haughty, unconcerned look, which didn't quite work with her red and swollen eyes. "That's absurd. It meant no more to me than it did to you."

"That's a lie. Cass, don't lie to me again. I don't care how much it hurts me or it hurts you, I want the truth."

"You've heard the truth a dozen times."

"I *said,* don't lie to me again." He spoke quietly but with an intensity that unnerved Cass.

"Are you threatening me?"

He smirked. "Hell, no. Where do you get these crazy ideas? Look, I'm the first one to admit what a horse's behind I was back then. I couldn't drive fast enough or drink enough, and I don't know why. I sure didn't get it from my folks. Maybe I'm a throwback to some harebrained ancestor." He waved his hand. "That's neither here nor there. I hurt you and that's all that's important. What I want to know, which I've asked you before, is why you went along with it that night. You said there was all kinds of force, and that's what I'm asking now. How did I force you?"

Heaving a sigh of utter misery, she dropped her head forward so she wouldn't have to look at him. "You didn't force me. How many times do you have to hear that before you believe it?"

"Okay, forget force. How about persuasion? Did I sweet-talk you into making love? Coerce you in some way? Cass, what did I do?"

The jig was up and Cass knew it. She had vowed to never have this conversation with anyone, least of all Gard. But from the determined look in his eyes, he wasn't going to accept anything else.

She crawled over to her cosmetic case and yanked out a handful of tissues, then returned to the bed to blow her nose and wipe her eyes.

"You're not going to leave me be until you hear it all, are you?" she said bitterly. "Do you care that talking about it will embarrass me?"

"No, I don't. And you want to know why? It's because you shouldn't be embarrassed about anything that ever happened between us, especially that old incident. Damn, Cass, I'm the one who should be embarrassed."

"Yeah, right," she said sarcastically. "Embarrassed by something you can't even remember."

"We've established and cursed my bad memory enough. Let's get to you. What were you doing at the dunes that night?"

She sucked in a breath. "I had every right to be there."

"Then you were there before me? What happened? Did I get there after you did? Was it planned? What I mean is, did we make a date to meet there?"

"A date!" she scoffed. "You didn't even know I was alive."

His eyes narrowed. "Then I went out there not knowing you were already there. I used to go to the dunes every so often, when I wanted to be alone."

"Same here."

"So you were there and I arrived, each of us looking for what? Some solitude?"

Cass's expression became a little sullen. "It's what I was looking for. I certainly can't speak for you."

"Okay, there we were, an accidental meeting. So, what happened?"

She rolled her eyes. "You know what happened."

"I came on to you?"

She was starting to feel choked. "Uh, I guess you could say that."

He leaned forward, his gaze boring into her. "Why did you let me?"

"Because..." She couldn't say it. She couldn't look at him and admit how much she had loved him. Or thought she had. Looking back, her feelings had been much more than a schoolgirl's crush, but love? She squared her shoulders. "I think I merely wanted to find out what sex was all about and you were handy."

Muttering a curse, he looked away. Then he brought his eyes back to her again, hard eyes, eyes brimming with doubt and disbelief. "That's another lie. Why can't you just admit that you liked me? Maybe you even loved me."

Anger exploded within her and she forgot all about embarrassing herself. "All right, here's the ugly truth, Rebel Sterling, and I hope you choke on it! I left the dunes that night stupid and starry-eyed, positive you were in love with me. It took about two weeks of waiting for you to call or come by the ranch, of seeing you on the street in town with barely a nod of recognition from you, before I finally realized that I meant nothing to you. No, that's not true. I did mean something... another easy mark, another notch on your bedpost. It hurt, damn you, it hurt so much I wanted to die."

"Cass," he said hoarsely, getting no joy from having figured out that she'd had strong feelings for him back then. "I'm sorry. What else can I say? I'm so damned sorry."

She was suddenly without anger, without emotion of any kind. "It doesn't matter anymore," she said, sounding weak and exhausted. It occurred to her, then, that it was true. Maybe finally telling him what he'd done had cleansed her soul, but whatever, she wasn't embarrassed about it and she was no longer angry. "Let's just forget it."

"I can't do that. Cass, I meant what I said in the pool. I love you."

"Oh, God, don't say that," she moaned. "Gard, I can't deal with your feelings now."

"What about your own feelings? Cassie, you didn't make love with me last night like a woman without feelings."

"I know," she whispered. "Can't you see how confused I am about it all?"

"You love me. I know you do."

She looked at him. "Then you know a lot more than I do."

"That's entirely possible." He got to his feet. "I'm going to break camp and take you home. But first I have to fix my truck."

"What's wrong with your truck?"

"Last night I got the bright idea of disabling it to keep you out here. I was going to pretend that I didn't know why it wouldn't start and put on a big show of working on it. But I think our game playing is over."

He took the few steps to the bed and knelt in front of her. "Cass, I knew right away that I wasn't going to buy your ranch. I couldn't, not without mortgaging my place to the hilt, which didn't make any sense."

He lifted his hand and tenderly brushed a lock of hair from her forehead. "But you see, when you walked into that banquet room, I felt like I'd been hit by a ton of bricks. And I'll answer your question, too. I've never been in love, not until seeing you again. I would have told you how I felt right away if you hadn't been so dead set against me. It really puzzled me, you know, why you didn't like me. I know I acted pretty foolishly about that option, having George send you those letters and all, but I couldn't think of any other way to get you to come back."

He smiled, one side of his mouth lifting higher than the other, a rather self-deprecating smile. "Remember one thing, all right? I'll always love you, no matter what. Maybe you'll get everything sorted out someday, and if you do, you know where to find me." Getting to his feet, he walked out.

Cass sat there feeling numb from her head to her toes. She could hear him moving around outside, but *she* honestly didn't have the strength to move.

Maybe you'll get everything sorted out someday, and if you do, you know where to find me.

Tears began dribbling down her cheeks again, and she just sat there and let them drip onto her blouse.

* * *

Packing up and loading the truck wasn't difficult, though it took several hours. The biggest problem was Cass's painting. Gard was speaking to her now as though that major confrontation in her tent had never occurred.

"The paint's still wet. We can't move it without some kind of cover."

Cass merely nodded. He might be able to go on as though nothing unusual had happened, but her whole body seemed to be one big ache.

Gard thought a minute. "I'll figure it out."

He did. Before her eyes he constructed a shipping crate out of odds and ends, including some pieces of tree limbs. It was a crude affair, but it worked, especially when he cut a length of canvas from his tarp and nailed it to the framework. That was when Cass found her voice.

"You've ruined your tarp."

"My tarp can be replaced. This painting can't," Gard said.

"Well . . . thank you," she mumbled, knowing she didn't sound nearly as grateful as she felt. But talking to him, even looking at him, was troubling.

When they were in the truck and ready to leave, Cass looked around. True to his word, Gard had left no evidence of their stay. Not so much as a tiny scrap of paper remained behind. Even the fire pit he had constructed had been dismantled and the ground leveled out. The area looked as though no one had ever been there, just as it had when they'd arrived.

She liked that about him, she thought as they headed out of the valley. She also liked his good humor, his looks, his intelligence and certainly his lovemaking. Her stomach sank. She *loved* his lovemaking. Oh, God, why couldn't she tell him that?

After a few miles, she also liked that he didn't seem inclined to make small talk. Apparently he understood that she wasn't feeling like chatting about nothing, and neither was he going to reopen their disturbing conversation in her tent.

Relaxing because of his silence, she settled back for the drive.

"Cass? We're here."

"Wha... Oh." It surprised her that she must have dozed. They were parked in her yard, with the truck's motor idling. "I must have fallen asleep."

"You did. Cass, will you remember one thing?" She tensed. "It's only this," Gard continued, ignoring the sudden tension he saw on her face. "If you feel like talking, or something, give me a call. I know you've got a lot to work through and you might need to talk along the way. I'll always be available."

She cleared her throat. "Thank you."

He opened his door. "I'll get your things."

For several days Cass stuck close to the house, walking the compound, wandering the rooms of her father's home, and thinking, thinking, thinking. The third day she saddled a horse for a ride.

Regardless that Gard was her most emotional problem, she had to make a decision about the ranch and gallery. At the very least she had to call Francis and bring her up-to-date. Maybe she would mention her abstracts, maybe she wouldn't, but Francis deserved the courtesy of a phone call, even if Cass hadn't yet come to any conclusions on that fifty percent buy-in.

But selling the ranch was beginning to feel crass and heartless. Riding along inhaling the sweet smell of alfalfa, soaking up the view of distant mountains and realizing that she was riding on Whitfield land nudged some very nostalgic memories. Her father putting her on a horse when she was very young. Her mother's face, laughing in the sunshine. The love between her parents. The love they'd both had for the ranch.

Cass's eyes got misty. If only they were still alive. They should be. They had both died too young. She needed them, desperately. Life wasn't fair.

But who had ever said it was? People made their own happiness, just as they caused their own unhappiness.

Sitting her horse on a rocky knoll that overlooked the Whitfield ranch, Cass's decision came to her, just as she had hoped it would, from out of nowhere and with sudden impact. She couldn't sell.

Drawing a deep breath, she nodded in satisfaction. She couldn't sell, which meant she couldn't buy into the gallery. Fine. She would call Francis as soon as she got back and relate her decision.

Now all she had to do was figure out what to do with her Oregon house.

Starting her horse down the trail from the overlook, she felt a weakening in her midsection. Her house in Oregon was small potatoes compared to her dilemma over Gard. He was in her every thought, just as he'd been fourteen years ago. She loved him, why not admit it? It was entirely possible that she had never *not* loved him.

What was constantly in her mind was that he loved her. Loved her enough to mention marriage. In his own way he had been fighting to get her attention since that day at the Plantation. What was stopping her from calling him, or going to his ranch? Was she still embarrassed, for pity's sake? Was she going to allow ancient embarrassment and humiliation to control the rest of her life? Maybe a part of her was still hurt because of his behavior so many years ago but, good grief, she wasn't a kid anymore, far from it, and clinging to that old incident was ridiculous.

Still...she couldn't quite picture herself with Gard and confessing her feelings. Maybe it would happen naturally, she thought. Maybe one day they would run into each other and...

Oh, Lord, what was wrong with her? Wasn't she beyond adolescent fantasizing?

Upon reaching the compound, Cass tended her horse and turned him out to pasture. Walking to the house, she slapped dust from her jeans. It hadn't rained here as it had that night in the valley and everything was dry and dusty. She stopped for a moment to scan the brilliant blue sky. Summer would soon be over, she thought with a touch of pathos. Before long they would have lots of rain, and then snow.

Sighing, she resumed her trek to the house. Going in, she heard Julia call, "Cass? I put the mail on your desk in the den."

"Thanks," Cass called back. She was thinking of a shower, but it could wait until she checked the mail.

In the den, she picked up the stack of mail and thumbed through it. A legal-size envelope with the Deering Gallery's return address stopped her. Laying down the other letters, she opened the one from Francis.

"Dear Ms. Whitfield."

Cass frowned. Francis usually called, but the few times she had written, she certainly hadn't addressed her so formally. Cass glanced down at the closing.

"Respectfully, Robert Beloit."

Who on earth was Robert Beloit? Cass returned to the body of the letter.

> I have been appointed by the court to attend to the Deering Gallery's inventory, and to inform you and many others of the current situation with the gallery.
>
> Francis Deering is under investigation for fraud. It appears that she sold fifty percent of her business to five different buyers. Both the money and Ms. Deering have vanished.
>
> Her inventory, of course, has been frozen by the court, except for the pieces that Ms. Deering held on consignment. As your work falls into that category, I

await your instructions as to its distribution. I see several options. You may personally pick up the pieces, I could send your work to another gallery, or I could ship it directly to you. Any cost incurred would have to be paid by you.

Please contact me as soon as possible regarding this matter.

Stunned, Cass sank onto the nearest chair. Francis had sold five fifty-percent shares? If she'd had the cash, would Francis have sold six shares?

"My God," Cass whispered. She had come very close to being taken to the cleaners. If Gard hadn't procrastinated on that option and she had succeeded in selling the ranch, Francis would have the proceeds and she, Cass, would have nothing. Obviously she hadn't known Francis at all. How could she have done such a terrible thing?

It took a while for Cass to assemble her thoughts. Then she dialed the Deering Gallery and spoke to Robert Beloit, requesting that he ship her paintings to Montana. They settled the details of cost and Cass hung up.

Then she sat back in her chair, feeling slightly shell-shocked. Her only problems now were her house in Oregon and Gard.

But Gard was not a problem, she suddenly realized. *She* was.

Grabbing a piece of notepaper and a pen, she wrote a message, slid the paper into an envelope, which she sealed and then wrote Gard's name on. Rising, she dashed through the house and out the back door, where she looked around for one of her hired hands. Spotting Rufe Biggins near the barn, she ran across the compound to where he was working.

"Rufe, would you please deliver this letter to Gard Sterling?"

Rufe nodded and took the envelope from Cass's hand. "I'll do it right now."

"Thanks, Rufe." She started to walk away, then stopped. "Rufe, make sure he gets it, okay? I mean, don't leave it with anyone else. It's crucial that he sees it today."

Gard watched Rufe climb into his pickup and drive away, then looked down at the envelope in his hand. He knew it was from Cass; Rufe had said so. But he was almost afraid to open it. If she had something to say to him, why had she written a letter rather than called?

Uneasily he finally tore the end from the envelope and extracted the letter. It was only a few lines, he saw, not a letter at all.

Gard,

I'm going to be at the dunes at ten o'clock tonight. Maybe you'd like to join me?

Cass

"Well, I'll be damned," he mumbled. Then a big grin broke out on his face. *Maybe you'd like to join me?* His smile got even bigger. It was clever of Cass to invite him to the dunes, where everything had begun for them. What else could he do now but hope that things were going to work out for them?

Whistling through his teeth, he got back to work. Ten o'clock was still a good six hours away.

Cass was at the dunes at quarter to ten. She arranged a large blanket on a pleasant curve in the sand, set out the small, insulated bag containing some cold soft drinks, and then sat down to wait. She would have liked to celebrate her change of attitude with champagne, but with Gard's aversion to alcohol, which she applauded, diet colas would have to do.

In a very few minutes she heard an approaching vehicle. Her heart immediately started beating double time, though she couldn't stop smiling. He had come, and she really hadn't been all that positive that he would.

Gard parked next to Cass's car and got out. Everything was dark and silent. "Cass?" he called.

"Up here, Gard."

He scanned the dunes and found her silhouette. "Be right there."

Cass sat down and waited with her heart thumping a mile a minute. He came trudging through the sand and stopped at the edge of her blanket. "Hi."

"Hi." She smiled. "Would you like to sit down?"

"Yes, thanks." He sat next to her. "Your note surprised me."

"I thought it might. I have some cold sodas with me. Would you like one?"

"Not now, but thanks."

"Um... I guess this is my show, right?"

"You've got me curious, that's for sure."

"Well... you told me if I wanted to talk that you'd be available."

"I meant it."

"I was sure you did. Uh, things have really been crazy. I learned today that the woman who owned the gallery I was planning to buy into sold the same fifty percent to five different people."

"She did what?"

"It's not important. I had already decided to keep the ranch and forget the gallery. You remember how I complained about having so many problems to deal with."

"And?"

"Well... now I've only got two."

Gard chuckled softly. "You sound disappointed."

"Oh, I'm not. Don't misunderstand. But the two I have left are...are... Well, one of them isn't unsolvable. I mean, I'm sure I can sell my house in Oregon with very little trouble. It's the other one that's—" she cleared her throat "—uh, been bothering me."

"And you think I can help? Cass, whatever it is, I'll do anything I can."

"I *know* you can help," she said softly, reaching for his hand. "You see, I have this awful ache right about here." She brought his hand to her lower abdomen.

Gard's pulse went wild. "I see." He, too, cleared his throat. "That's a problem, all right, a serious problem. An ache in that area can drive a person over the edge in no time."

"Yes, I believe you're right." She inched closer and cast him a sideways glance. "Gard...I...I..."

"Say it, honey. It won't hurt, I promise."

She could barely breathe. "I...I love you."

He let go of a huge lungful of air. "Thank you, God." Catching her in a feverish embrace, he brought them both down to the blanket. His kisses fell everywhere, on her nose, her forehead, her lips. "I love you so much I can't see straight."

"Me, too," she whispered raggedly. "Gard, look at me."

He lifted his head. "I'm looking, baby."

"Do you still want to marry me?"

"You bet I do. The sooner the better."

She smiled impishly. "Okay. You don't have to look at me anymore. You can get on with the kissing and other stuff now. Please take note that I brought a blanket for the occasion."

He kissed her hard and passionately, then laid his hand on her stomach. "Have you really had an ache in here?"

"An unbearable ache. Fix it, my love. You're the only one who can."

"Gladly, sweetheart, gladly."

Epilogue

It seemed that the happy couple had one more problem. After all, they had two ranches, each with a very nice home. The subject came up for discussion two days before their wedding.

"Where would you like to live?" Gard asked.

"Where would *you* like to live?"

"Cass, let me tell you what's important to me, all right? Before anything else, your happiness. I can be equally contented in my house or yours. Hell, I could be contented living in a cave if you were there with me. So, you see, it has to be your decision."

"Hmm," Cass murmured. "Well, do you think we should sell one of the ranches?"

"Why would we do that?"

"Because I'd like to spend my time painting. That would put the burden of both ranches on you, and I'd hate seeing you working yourself into exhaustion day after day."

Gard laughed and kissed her. "Thanks for the consideration, sweetheart, but I can run two ranches as easy as one. Cass, I want you to paint. It would be criminal if someone with your talent didn't use it. Leave the ranches to me, okay?"

"If you're sure."

"I'm sure. That's settled, but we still haven't decided where to live."

Cass thought for a few moments. "I can't decide."

"All right, then we'll live in both houses."

She looked at him and started laughing. "Now that makes a lot of sense."

"What the hell? It just isn't important, Cass. We'll figure it out. Com'ere." He brought her head to his shoulder. "Know what I've been thinking about?"

"What?"

"That document between our fathers. Neither of them was a stupid man, Cass. In fact, they were both way above average in intelligence. They had to have known that you and I would have to deal with their buy/sell option someday. Do you suppose they hoped it would bring us together?"

Startled, Cass sat up. "I never thought of that. You know, they could have limited that option to their lifetime."

"They sure could have. Instead, they left it in so you and I would have to figure out what to do with it." He chuckled. "Cagey old guys, huh?"

"The best cagey old guys there ever was, Gard."

He nodded. "The very best, sweetheart."

* * * * *

SILHOUETTE® *Desire*®

COMING NEXT MONTH

#967 A COWBOY CHRISTMAS—Ann Major

Born under the same Christmas star, December's *Man of the Month,* Leander Knight, and sexy Heddy Kinney shared the same destiny. Now the handsome cowboy had to stop her holiday wedding—to *another* man!

#968 MIRACLES AND MISTLETOE—Cait London

Rugged cowboy Jonah Fargo was a Scrooge when it came to Christmas—until Harmony Davis sauntered into his life. Could she get him under the mistletoe and make him believe in miracles?

#969 COWBOYS DON'T STAY—Anne McAllister

Code of the West

Tess Montgomery had fallen for Noah Tanner years ago, but he left her with a broken heart *and* a baby. Now that he was back, could he convince her that sometimes cowboys do stay?

#970 CHRISTMAS WEDDING—Pamela Macaluso

Just Married

Holly Bryant was expected to pose as Jesse Tyler's bride-to-be, not fall for the hardheaded man! But Jesse was a woman's dream come true, even though he swore he'd never settle down....

#971 TEXAS PRIDE—Barbara McCauley

Hearts of Stone

Jessica Stone didn't need help from anyone, especially a lone wolf like Dylan Grant. But Dylan refused to let Jessica's Texas pride—and her to-die-for looks—stand in his way!

#972 GIFT WRAPPED DAD—Sandra Steffen

Six-year-old Tommy Wilson asked Santa for a dad, so he was thrilled when Will Sutherland showed up in time for Christmas. Now if only Will could convince Tommy's mom he'd make the perfect husband for her!

MILLION DOLLAR SWEEPSTAKES (III)

No purchase necessary. To enter, follow the directions published. Method of entry may vary. For eligibility, entries must be received no later than March 31, 1996. No liability is assumed for printing errors, lost, late or misdirected entries. Odds of winning are determined by the number of eligible entries distributed and received. Prizewinners will be determined no later than June 30, 1996.

Sweepstakes open to residents of the U.S. (except Puerto Rico), Canada, Europe and Taiwan who are 18 years of age or older. All applicable laws and regulations apply. Sweepstakes offer void wherever prohibited by law. Values of all prizes are in U.S. currency. This sweepstakes is presented by Torstar Corp., its subsidiaries and affiliates, in conjunction with book, merchandise and/or product offerings. For a copy of the Official Rules send a self-addressed, stamped envelope (WA residents need not affix return postage) to: MILLION DOLLAR SWEEPSTAKES (III) Rules, P.O. Box 4573, Blair, NE 68009, USA.

EXTRA BONUS PRIZE DRAWING

No purchase necessary. The Extra Bonus Prize will be awarded in a random drawing to be conducted no later than 5/30/96 from among all entries received. To qualify, entries must be received by 3/31/96 and comply with published directions. Drawing open to residents of the U.S. (except Puerto Rico), Canada, Europe and Taiwan who are 18 years of age or older. All applicable laws and regulations apply; offer void wherever prohibited by law. Odds of winning are dependent upon number of eligibile entries received. Prize is valued in U.S. currency. The offer is presented by Torstar Corp., its subsidiaries and affiliates in conjunction with book, merchandise and/or product offering. For a copy of the Official Rules governing this sweepstakes, send a self-addressed, stamped envelope (WA residents need not affix return postage) to: Extra Bonus Prize Drawing Rules, P.O. Box 4590, Blair, NE 68009, USA.

SWP-S1195

Silhouette
SPECIAL EDITION®

CELEBRATION 1000

It's our 1000th Special Edition and we're celebrating!

Join us these coming months for some wonderful stories in a special celebration of our 1000th book with some of your favorite authors!

Diana Palmer
Debbie Macomber
Phyllis Halldorson
Nora Roberts
Christine Flynn
Lisa Jackson

Plus miniseries by:

Lindsay McKenna, Marie Ferrarella, Sherryl Woods and Gina Ferris Wilkins.

And many more books by special writers!

And as a special bonus, all Silhouette Special Edition titles published during Celebration 1000! will have ***double*** Pages & Privileges proofs of purchase!

Silhouette Special Edition...heartwarming stories packed with emotion, just for you! You'll fall in love with our next 1000 special stories!

1000BK-R

Who needs mistletoe when Santa's Little Helpers are around?

Santa's Little Helpers

brought to you by:

Janet Dailey
Jennifer Greene
Patricia Gardner Evans

This holiday collection has three contemporary stories celebrating the joy of love during Christmas. Featuring a BRAND-NEW story from *New York Times* bestselling author Janet Dailey, this special anthology makes the perfect holiday gift for you or a loved one!

FREE GIFT
with purchase
see inside

You can receive a beautiful 18″ goldtone rope necklace—absolutely FREE—with the purchase of ***Santa's Little Helpers.*** See inside the book for details.

Santa's Little Helpers—a holiday gift you will want to open again and again!

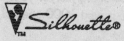

Silhouette® TM

SLH95

Three brothers...
Three proud, strong men who live—and love—by

THE CODE OF THE WEST

Meet the Tanner brothers—Robert, Luke, and now, Noah—in Anne McAllister's

COWBOYS DON'T STAY
(December, Desire #969)

Tess Montgomery had fallen for Noah Tanner years ago—but he left her with a broken heart *and* a baby. Now he was back, but could he convince her that sometimes cowboys do stay?

Only from

SILHOUETTE® Desire®

COW2

SILHOUETTE®
Desire®
Hearts of Stone

Three strong-willed Texas siblings whose rock-hard protective walls are about to come tumblin' down!

The Silhouette Desire miniseries by

BARBARA McCAULEY

concludes in December 1995 with

TEXAS PRIDE (Silhouette Desire #971)

Raised with a couple of overprotective brothers, Jessica Stone *hated* to be told what to do. So when her sexy new foreman started trying to run her life, Jessica's pride said she had to put a stop to it. But her heart said something *entirely* different....

HOS3

You're About to Become a Privileged Woman

Reap the rewards of fabulous free gifts and benefits with proofs-of-purchase from Silhouette and Harlequin books

Pages & Privileges™

It's our way of thanking you for buying our books at your favorite retail stores.

PROOF OF PURCHASE SD-PP75
Offer expires October 31,1996

Pages & Privileges™

**Harlequin and Silhouette—
the most privileged readers in the world!**

For more information about Harlequin and Silhouette's PAGES & PRIVILEGES program call the Pages & Privileges Benefits Desk: 1-503-794-2499

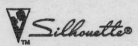

Silhouette®

SD-PP75